SLOW BIRTH

(Heat of Love, Book 2.5)

LETA BLAKE

An Original Publication from Leta Blake Books

Slow Birth (Heat of Love #2.5)
Written and published by Leta Blake
Cover by Dar Albert
Formatted by BB eBooks

First Edition, 2019
Print Edition

ISBN: 979-8-88841-004-2

Other Books by Leta Blake

Contemporary

Will & Patrick Wake Up Married
Will & Patrick's Endless Honeymoon
Cowboy Seeks Husband
The Difference Between
Bring on Forever
Stay Lucky

Sports

The River Leith

The Training Season Series
Training Season
Training Complex

Musicians

Smoky Mountain Dreams
Vespertine

New Adult

Punching the V-Card

Winter Holidays

The Home for the Holidays Series
Mr. Frosty Pants
Mr. Naughty List
Mr. Jingle Bells

Fantasy

Any Given Lifetime

Re-imagined Fairy Tales

Flight
Levity

Paranormal & Shifters

Angel Undone
Omega Mine

Horror

Raise Up Heart

Omegaverse

Heat of Love Series
Slow Heat
Alpha Heat
Slow Birth
Bitter Heat

For Sale Series
Heat for Sale

Coming of Age

'90s Coming of Age Series
Pictures of You
You Are Not Me

Audiobooks

Leta Blake at Audible

Discover more about the author online

Leta Blake
letablake.com

Gay Romance Newsletter

Leta's newsletter will keep you up to date on her latest releases and news from the world of M/M romance. Join the mailing list today. letablake.com

Leta Blake on Patreon

Become part of Leta Blake's Patreon community in order to access exclusive content, deleted scenes, extras, bonus stories, rewards, prizes, interviews, and more. www.patreon.com/letablake

Acknowledgements

Thank you to the following:

Patreon and all of my patrons there. I wrote this as a gift for them, and I hope all readers of this series enjoy it, too!

Mom & Dad

Brian & Cecily

Kim V for her friendship and understanding

Keira Andrews for her generous friendship and handholding on the regular

A.M. Arthur for loving *the Heat of Love universe* so much that she made up her own Omegaverse books. Look for *Breaking Free*!

Devon Vesper for her dedication to this series and this book, and for her outstanding editing work

And thank you to my readers who make all the blood, sweat, and tears of writing worthwhile! You all have my heart!

Jason and Vale are back in this side story set in the Heat of Love universe!

A romantic getaway turns dramatic when an unexpected heat descends on Vale, leaving Jason with no choice but to act.

The resulting pregnancy is dangerous for Vale and terrifying for Jason, but with the help of friends and family, they choose to embrace their uncertain future. Together they find all the love, joy, and heat they need to guide them through!

While this story follows the characters from *Slow Heat*, it will be most enjoyed if read directly after *Alpha Heat*, as it takes place contemporaneously with that story.

For my passionate patrons

PART ONE

Mountain Heat

CHAPTER ONE

T HE CABIN LOOKED almost nothing like Vale remembered it. The swing on the front porch he'd enjoyed as a child was still there, and the slope in the back he'd gone sledding down more than once was as steep as ever, but everything else about his parents' old retreat in the mountains had undergone a complete overhaul in every way.

Vale's mouth hung open as he walked through the main rooms of the remodeled chalet. The renovators made the windows bigger, the doors taller, and the furniture more luxurious than his parents could have ever afforded. The appliances in the kitchen were even nicer even than the new ones Jason had installed in their home back in the city.

"Do you like it?" Jason asked, swooping in behind Vale with their overnight bags and a kiss to the back of his neck. "Is it too much?"

"No, it's…" Vale trailed off, unable to wrangle a word to describe the place, which was pretty sad for a professor of literature and a published poet. He huffed and rubbed at his arms.

"Too fancy?"

"It's lovely."

Vale's in-laws—Jason's parents, the Sabel-Hoffs—had money and taste. Two things Vale's parents (wolf-god keep them both) had definitely lacked. Vale liked to think of his and Jason's cluttered home on Oak Avenue as quaint, but if he were honest, it was just a mess.

This renovation was the work of the Sabel-Hoffs, and while he couldn't complain about any aspect, it was a little bittersweet, nonetheless. It didn't feel like it was his anymore. And, most likely, it wouldn't be for long. This was a final trip to say goodbye before they placed the chalet on the market and the funds from the sale deposited in an account that was ostensibly Vale's. Though technically, it, like everything of his since they contracted, would be Jason's.

As Vale stood aimlessly in the living room, gazing at the familiar view, Jason moved deeper into the chalet to put their things away in the master bedroom. Vale wasn't sure he was ready to look quite yet. His parents' old, rundown bed, rocker, and chest of drawers would be long gone, and his old little room, which had consisted of a twin bed with a star quilt, would have been overhauled, too.

He wondered what had become of the quilt.

"So?" Jason said, returning to the living room emptyhanded with a worried expression on his face. "Talk to me. We don't have to sell it, you know. If you want to, if you like it, or it's important to you, then we can keep it. Just say the word."

Vale rubbed his arms again. The air in the cabin was cold, and yet he felt hot. Emotions did weird things like that, he found. "Everything's so new. There isn't even any dust yet."

"If we keep the place," Jason said with a wink, "I'm sure you can easily change that."

Vale stuck out his tongue like a child. Housekeeping wasn't his forte, no. But neither of them enjoyed having beta servants in their space. Jason hadn't grown up that way, and neither had Vale, so they were on the same page as far as that went. Which also meant they lived in a grimy state of moderate disrepair by Jason's parents' standards—fine, by most of society's standards. But they were happy, so neither of them particularly cared.

"Vale," Jason whispered, stepping closer. "Did we go too far?

Change it too much?"

Vale shook off his maudlin feelings and gave Jason a smile that went far to relieve his baby alpha's worry. "Nonsense. It's beautiful. It was a rundown hovel before. Take me back to the bedrooms. I'd like to see the changes there."

Jason's fingers were warm and strong as he took Vale's hand and tugged him along the hallway. "This way, then."

Originally there'd been three rooms at the back of the chalet. One had been Vale's small room, a second had been used as his father's office when they summered up here, and the third had been the master bedroom—the domain of his father and pater, boasting the best views of the mountains.

"We combined these two rooms," Jason said, motioning to his right. "They were both so small by today's standards that the architect thought it would be easier to sell the place if we combined them for a bigger space."

He opened the door, and Vale peered in. The far side of the room would have been his original bedroom, and he saw that the renovators removed the rose wallpaper his pater had put up for him when he was young. The side of the room closer to the door featured a big window that his father's desk used to sit under, though it, too, had been enlarged. They had painted the walls a bright, clear cream color, and the space fairly glowed with the light coming in from the windows. There was a bed, also with cream coverlets, and a modern chest of drawers along with a matching desk, table, and a mint green settee completing the space. Simple, lovely. Nothing like his old summer home.

"Beautiful," he murmured again before pulling his head back out and straightening his shoulders, steeling himself for the next bit.

"And this way is the master bedroom, of course. We'll stay in here."

Vale stepped into the room this time and blinked at the change.

The window that overlooked the most spectacular view now took up the whole wall. The entire back section of the cottage had been removed to allow maximum exposure to the glorious whitecapped mountains and the crystal blue lake.

He sucked in a breath, almost unable to draw his eyes away until Jason swept his hand around the room and said, "This is where we'll sleep tonight."

Vale pressed a hand to his mouth as he took in the big bed. Not his parents' bed, that's for sure, but in the middle of it was his old star quilt, worked into a larger quilt that covered the massive mattress. "Oh. That's my…"

"I know," Jason said, touching Vale's shoulder. "We'll take that with us when we go. Unless you want to keep this place, and then I guess it can stay."

"You thought of that?" Vale wasn't surprised. Jason was the most thoughtful of alphas.

"No, Pater did. But I thought it was a great idea when he mentioned it. We'd come up together to see what he thought regarding the place's potential, and he spotted the quilt on what must have been your bed. He thought you might like to have it."

Vale smiled. Miner was a good pater-in-law, even if he was sometimes annoyingly demanding of Jason's time. But who wouldn't be? Jason was perfect and wonderful. Vale was demanding of Jason's time, too. "Thank him for me."

Finally, he tore his eyes away from the quilt and looked around the rest of the room. Miner had clearly had his hand in this as well. The furniture was expensive, modern, and perfectly tasteful. Aside from the big bed, there was an armoire, a tan chaise lounge, a writing desk, and a vanity with a mirror.

"The bathroom got an overhaul, too," Jason said, opening the en suite door and flipping on the light. "A big tub and a natural shower."

Vale saw what Jason meant by natural when he entered to find that, like in the bedroom, an entire wall of the bathroom was now glass. A sliding glass door in the shower allowed someone to open it and step naked into nature if they wanted. Vale laughed under his breath. Of the two of them, he was more likely to use that feature. Though, perhaps not this trip. The weather was already so chilly.

He lifted his shirt and let in a waft of that cold air, hoping he cooled down soon.

"The laundry is behind the kitchen, and we added a separate outbuilding for all the storage."

"It's stunning," Vale said, taking Jason's hand and pulling him out of the bathroom and down the hallway. "Let's get the groceries in before they spoil, and then we can take a walk around the property. I can show you all my old haunts."

"I'd love that." Jason lifted Vale's hand to his mouth and kissed his fingers. "I want to see everything from your point of view."

Vale turned at the doorway and pulled Jason close. "And I want to share it all with you."

Every day with Jason was new and beautiful. They rarely argued and still desperately fucked. He knew that *Érosgápe* were obsessed with each other in ways few other humans could understand. But now he knew for himself how beautiful it could be, and he couldn't imagine the emptiness of living any other way.

Jason's scent, his laugh, his very way of breathing made Vale tingle with lust and shake with love, and when they came together physically, the world meant nothing outside of the pleasure they took in each other's arms.

Bittersweet or not, being at the cabin with Jason more than made up for any sense of loss he had in the changes made. Being with Jason was always perfect.

JASON LOVED THE way the cool air made Vale's pale skin pink up. His *Érosgápe's* cheeks were rosy, and his eyes glowed as they finished their trek around the mountain property.

"The lake was always too far to go alone," Vale was saying. They followed the winding path of the babbling spring that led down to the bright blue waters below. The trees overhung the area with fading green leaves, autumn coming on soon. "But I played in this brook all the time. I'd turn over the rocks looking for creatures. I bet little Jason would have loved to play here with me."

"He would have." Jason loved playing anywhere with Vale *now*.

Vale knelt beside the fresh stream and took the clear water into his palms and splashed his face and beard. He gasped when the shock of the water soaked into his beard and grinned up at Jason. "Here, you do it."

"No way. It's freezing out here as it is." Jason laughed and held Vale's coat out to him. "Put this back on before you catch your death."

"You're acting like your pater," Vale said with a wink. Then he frowned. "You're really not hot at all?"

"No! It's cold as wolf's own hell, and you're being ridiculous. Here." He shook the coat at Vale again.

Vale slid it on but didn't button it, his brow furrowing thoughtfully.

"What?"

"We're going back to the city tomorrow?" Vale asked, looking up at the sky and then around at the tall, creaking trees.

"That was the plan. But if you want to stay a few days, we can."

"No," Vale said quickly. "I think it's best if we go back tomorrow."

"Oh." Jason didn't exactly know why, but he felt a bit crestfallen. It was only now, in this exact moment, that he realized he'd held out hope that Vale would fall in love with the work on the cabin and they could stay to fuck sweetly for a few days—a second bonding-moon of sorts—and returning for sexy vacations throughout the year. He knew Vale loved the sea as much as he did, but whenever they went on those trips, so many others insisted on coming along. He'd imagined this place as a retreat for just the two of them.

Vale, of course, sensed his change of mood and turned, taking his hand. His palm was rather warm, but it was probably from all the walking. Vale was a sedentary sort, usually. It was remarkable he managed to stay so trim. Good genes probably. "It's beautiful, and I want to come back," Vale said. "It's just that there's business I need to attend to in the city."

"What kind of business?" Jason asked.

Vale shrugged. "I'm not sure."

A bear then lumbered out of the woods only a short distance away, and Jason grabbed Vale, placing a hand over his mouth to keep him quiet. They stared intently at the bear as it lumbered into the stream, took a drink, and then headed off in the opposite direction from the house.

"I can't believe your pater and father let you play alone out there when there are bears!" Jason said when they'd safely reached the house again.

"I don't remember seeing any when I was young," Vale said. He laughed and immediately pulled his coat off as soon as the door was open. He slung it over a chair as was his wont, and Jason scooped it up to hang on the coat rack by the door. "I must have been too loud and scared them off with all my fantasy games."

Jason gathered Vale close, relief and anxiety threading together. "You're safe," he reassured Vale. Though, really, he was reassuring himself.

Vale kissed his neck. "Oh, baby alpha, you're so sweet."

"Do that again, and we won't have dinner for hours," Jason murmured, sliding his hands down to cup Vale's ass. "I've wanted to get you out of these clothes and see how your body likes the fresh air ever since we arrived."

"See how my body likes the fresh air?" Vale laughed again. "I'm sure my body is exactly the same as when I arrived."

"I think I should make sure, don't you? I'm not sure fresh air and exercise agrees with my couch-loving omega," Jason said, starting on the buttons of Vale's shirt. He slid it off Vale's shoulders, and then tugged Vale's undershirt off, too. "Mmm, so beautiful."

He slid his hands over Vale's skin, rubbing over the tattoos and tweaking his nipples. Vale squirmed but stepped closer instead of drawing away. Jason grinned. "You like that."

"I love it."

"Yes." Jason bent to kiss Vale's neck, his scent strongest there, and shuddered at the sweet, ripening smell of his *Érosgápe's* arousal and slick. "I smell you opening for me."

"Always, darling."

Jason shuddered and kissed Vale's throat. "Let's go to the bedroom."

Vale voiced no argument for that. Clearly, he agreed that food could wait. Vale frowned softly, though, and shivered. "We'll go home tomorrow?" he asked again.

"If you want." Jason took hold of Vale's nipples, pinching gently, and then used them to lead Vale down the hallway to the bedroom. The slight pain of the tug was evident in the small grimace that came and went on Vale's face, but his arousal was also evident in the way his hips bucked forward slightly, and the scent of pre-cum and slick rose all around them.

Vale opened his mouth to speak, but Jason wasn't in the mood to talk now. He wanted to screw and suck and fuck. He pinched Vale's nipples rather hard and smiled as Vale tossed his head back on a gasp, stumbling forward. The scent of slick grew thick, and Jason laughed softly as he kicked open the master bedroom door, fingers still tormenting Vale's red nubs. He led Vale to the giant bed, both of their pants distended by erections, and any thought of conversation slid away.

"Dinner?" Vale whispered, but his trembling body and reaching hands gave away that he had no desire to stop what they were doing to prepare a meal together right now.

"Fuck dinner," Jason muttered darkly. "I'm going to eat you instead."

"Oh, darling, you say the sweetest things."

CHAPTER TWO

VALE HAD LONG been a fan of fucking and had little shame about that. He'd told Jason when they met that he was highly motivated by sex, and it hadn't been a lie. But when it came to sex with Jason, Vale wasn't just a fan. He was an addict. He truly could not get enough and would give up food, fun, friends, and anything resembling work to stay home, get naked, and spend his hours coming for Jason.

"Twice already?" Jason asked, laughing as he fucked into Vale's ass, shouldering Vale's thighs and bending him nearly in half. "You're so easy, baby."

"You're so good." Vale gasped and shuddered as Jason's thrust filled him up and pressed perfectly against his omega glands and prostate. He'd already ejaculated twice, and he felt so close to an anal orgasm that he was already bracing for it. A few more thrusts and he was there, aching and twitching as he convulsed on Jason's dick.

"Oh, fuck, baby, that's gorgeous. Look at you come," Jason murmured, not slowing his hips at all, pounding into Vale like he wasn't already in ecstasy and needed something more to push him over. "Don't stop. Don't fucking stop coming for me."

Vale couldn't if he'd tried. He was at the mercy of his body now, and the ecstatic talons of keen pleasure had him. The convulsions went on and on, and as soon as they stopped, another thrust set them off again. Jason stared down at him with wide, adoring eyes. Vale never felt more beautiful than when he was coming apart on Jason's cock, covered in sweat, cum, and slick.

Time dissolved and resolved around punctuations of intense bliss. When Vale finally thought he'd lose his mind from pleasure and begged to Jason to fill him with cum, Jason slammed in deep, held tight, and cried out his climax.

"Oh, darling, fill me up," Vale whimpered. "Give me your babies." It was raunchy omega bed talk. Arousing, yes, but also tender and full of longing because it was a plea he could never fulfill. Vale had internal scars, and a baby could never grow in him—not without risking his life.

Jason shook and cursed, kissing Vale's neck and shoulder as the orgasm dragged out. Young and full of spunk, he could shoot quite a huge load, and soon the excess spilled out of Vale and slid down his ass crack, adding to the wetness of the bed.

Exhausted and still annoyingly aroused, Vale vaguely hoped there were plenty of clean sheets and blankets, because it looked like it was going to be a cold night, and they'd already messed up this set. Though here in Jason's arms, he was plenty warm. He groaned as Jason pulled out of him and pressed kisses all over his chest, down his sternum, and then his ticklish belly. He huffed a chuckle.

"Let me clean you, and then I'll make dinner."

Vale had no idea how Jason had the energy for that after he'd walked all over the property with Vale, fucked him for an hour, and shot into Vale hard enough to fill him to the brim. But Vale wasn't going to protest, though he didn't feel particularly hungry. "I'm tired, darling," he whispered as Jason wiped him down with a warm washcloth and tended to his slick ass.

"Nap, then. Dinner will take some time to prepare," Jason said, pulling a warm robe around Vale's shoulders. "Here, this side of the bed is dry. I'll change the sheets later."

Vale scooted over to the other side of the big mattress, the one closest to the windows. Then after Jason kissed his forehead, praised his tight ass once more, and made sure he was warm, Jason left Vale alone to stare out at the fading light on the trees and lake below. The bed was colder near the window, but it felt good. Vale opened his robe and lifted the blankets that Jason had so carefully bundled him in, and let his hot skin take in the coolness. He smiled, tweaking his own nipples, and thinking about the way Jason's eyes always went so sweet and vulnerable just before he came. The most intimate gaze imaginable. Vale loved being the one to make his baby alpha feel that way.

As his eyes grew heavier, the inevitable nap drawing him down, Vale noticed flurries begin to fall beyond the window. It was early for snow, so despite how pretty it was, he knew there was no hope of it sticking or being more than a quick snow shower. Drowsing, he remembered when he and Jason had first met, there'd been a night when snow had threatened, and Jason had promised to take Vale sledding the next day if it did.

The snow hadn't stuck that time, and the sledding had never happened, but that sweet night was still a cherished memory. After all, his baby alpha *had* stuck, even if the snow hadn't. And Jason was the best thing that had ever happened in Vale's life. Better even than the night he'd found out that his first book of poems was to be published. It astonished him now to remember that he'd thought that moment the pinnacle of potential joy. It came nowhere near even a simple morning spent with Jason. Waking by his side, breathing his scent, watching him putter in the garden at their house, or get ready for his day at work. These were all true pinnacles for Vale.

Vale was happy, beyond anything he'd ever deserved, and he could only imagine that these beautiful moments would one day become mundane to him. But not yet. He thought there were still a few surprises in store for him and Jason. He just didn't know what exactly they might be.

But when he woke an hour and a half later, he was shocked to find that a freak snowstorm in the middle of autumn was one of them.

That, and something much more ominous.

Because in Vale's sleep, he'd thrown every stitch off and still he felt way too hot. Pinpricks of heat danced under his skin. Worse, his body ached with that tell-tale yearning which heralded a rapidly approaching heat.

"Jason," he called, his stomach rolling slightly at the delicious scent of food in the air. Repulsion toward food…another sign of heat. Heart beating hard, he got to his feet and tugged the robe on, walking down the hallway toward the kitchen noises. "Jason?"

Brightly lit, the living room glowed from the electric lights running off the new-fangled generator that Jason had shown him as they'd walked around the property earlier. Jason had the radio turned to some classical music like his pater listened to in his conservatory, and he slowly moved around the kitchen from pot to pot, lifting and stirring, and smiling at his work.

"Jason?"

Jason turned to him with such a beautiful expression that Vale hated to know what he was about to say would wipe it away. "Oh, good," Jason said. "You're awake. The food's almost done. Just a few more minutes."

"I'm so sorry, darling, but we have to go home. Now."

"What? Why?" Jason tilted his head, and the motioned toward the large windows. "Vale, it's snowing. It's coming down in wet clumps. We can't go home tonight. I doubt we can go home tomorrow, even. I'm sorry." He grinned and winked. "But that means we can play more."

Vale's knees went weak, but he managed to stumble to the front door of the cottage and open it up, unwilling to take the view out the windows as proof. Sure enough, the open sky that had been visible before he fell asleep was now dark, no moon in sight. Thick clouds let loose fat, wet snowflakes the size of silver pieces. It had accumulated quickly, already covering the path and the driveway.

"Vale?" Jason came up behind him then, worry in his voice. He pressed along Vale's back and hooked his chin over Vale's shoulder, peering out into the eerie white darkness. "See? It's going to be impassable before long, if it isn't already, and it's way too dangerous to try to drive in this mess tonight. What's wrong?" He turned Vale around and took hold of his chin so that he could peer down into his eyes.

The door was still ajar, and the cold air felt amazing on Vale's hot skin. He was tempted to open the robe but knew that would distress Jason, and what he had to say was going to distress him enough. "Don't panic," Vale said slowly. Though *he* was panicking even now. His breath came in gulps, and his heart pounded so hard he felt faint. "Whatever happens, don't panic."

Jason's eyes went wide, and he shut the door before guiding Vale to the sofa and pushing him down on it. "What's wrong? Are you sick?" He put his fingers on Vale's forehead. "You're burning up."

"My heat," Vale muttered. "It's early."

"What? No. That's not possible. You just had it two months ago."

"Apparently it is, Jason, because it's happening right now. I'm hot all over, inside and out, and I'm old enough to know what these feelings mean. I've been through these enough times now."

Jason swallowed hard. "Fuck."

"We need to go home."

"We can't," Jason whispered. "The weather is…" Then he squeezed his eyes shut. "I only have a couple of condoms with me. In the First Aid kit. I didn't think this could happen."

"We have to try," Vale said. He stood up and headed toward

the door again. "Turn off the stove and the oven, leave everything else. If we go right now—"

A big crash of thunder rolled, and a flash of lightning illuminated every shadow in the room. It was followed almost immediately by a cracking noise—a splintering that made him fear something had struck the house—and then a huge thumping bang shook the room. Jason turned back to the front door, jerked it open and stared in shock. "A tree fell across the drive. And on our car."

Vale stood up, his legs quivering, and with his heart pounding, he stepped up by Jason and peered out into the night. The tree was massive, the car ruined.

"Call your parents," Vale whispered. "They can come get us. We can walk part of the way down to meet them."

"Even if that was safe, and even if they could make it up the mountain in this snowstorm, the phones are down, babe."

"Down?"

"The storm knocked them out about an hour ago. I noticed when I tried to call my parents to let them know we'd arrived safely. All it takes is a branch on the line anywhere along the mountain to do it."

"No." Vale wrapped his arms around himself, scratching at his arms. The heat prickled even harder as the cool air rushed inside, obliterating the warmth from the fire Jason had laid.

Jason pulled him into his arms and kissed the top of his head. "Let's think. There has to be a solution. I have two condoms. I could use each one more than once until they…until they break."

"Jason, you don't understand. I'm going into heat. We're talking *days* of constant fucking." Vale broke free and walked out onto the front porch and began to pace its length, watching as the snow piled ever deeper, moment by moment. "I have to get out of here. We can't be trapped. We need condoms. We need to be safe!"

"Don't you think I know that?" Jason snapped, and then wiped a hand over his face, and his tone turned contrite and scared. "I know, okay? But what are we going to do?" He tugged Vale back into the cabin, shutting the door to keep in the warmth.

Vale flung himself down on the sofa and rubbed his temples. "There's a neighbor. Or there was. Maybe he has a working phone, or condoms, or both."

"How far is he?" Jason asked, already pulling on his coat. He headed into the kitchen and turned off all the burners and the oven, too. Vale watched him with wide eyes. "Which direction? I'll go. You wait here."

"I don't remember his name. But he lived down-mountain, and my parents would get honey from him when it was in season." Vale explained the way down to Jason and then said, "We'll both go."

"No," Jason barked with more authority than he often used outside the bedroom. "You'll wait here and eat the dinner I made. I don't care if you're not hungry, you'll eat it to gain strength for whatever is ahead. If we have to weather a heat here, I want you healthy. If we have to walk down the mountain to meet help, I want you fueled for that, too. Do you understand me? Eat the food."

Vale's stomach jolted warningly at the idea, but he nodded. His alpha commanded so he'd do what he could. "I don't want you going alone. What if you get lost?"

"I'll be fine," Jason said, grabbing a flashlight and a hat, too, a grim set to his face. "Stay here. I'll be back."

The door shut on Jason's back and Vale wished he'd gotten a kiss before he'd left. What if something terrible happened? What if Jason didn't return?

Vale sat down at the kitchen table with a bowl of soft-cooked vegetables and a plate of mashed potatoes—the only items Vale thought he could begin to stomach—and he ate it slowly as the oncoming heat swelled and released and worry ate at his heart.

CHAPTER THREE

J ASON WAS SOAKED through, cold and miserable, and the house he'd finally located down-mountain from their cabin was empty. Not just empty of human life, but empty of anything. Whoever had lived there had moved out long ago and taken everything with him.

He turned around, helpless and frustrated, and trudged back the way he'd come. The snow had continued to dump from the sky, covering his footprints and obscuring his way. He had to pay strict attention not to miss the turns and twists he needed to take to return to the chalet. Panic held him in its grasp, and he could barely admire the beauty of the eerily bright world of white he stumbled through.

By the time he reached the driveway leading to Vale's cabin again, his nose, feet, and hands were completely numb, and he was chilled bone-deep. As he approached, a deeper kind of chill went up his spine, and he found the energy to run ahead.

Vale was screaming.

Fuck. The heat had come on so fast. Jason had never seen anything like it. Though he'd heard rumors, of course, about older omegas having unexpected heats as they came near the end of their fertile years—especially those who'd endured rebound heats after trying heat suppressants. Urho had told him of a recent study, even, that spelled out a connection between the two. A warning that Jason really should have taken to heart. But he hadn't. Vale always seemed so beautiful and perfect to him. He forgot most of the time that Vale was so much older.

"Baby, no, no. Oh, no," Jason said, thrusting the door open. He found Vale already naked and shaking—torso on the sofa, knees on the floor, ass up, and the most pained scream coming from his throat. "I'm here. I'm here," he said, tearing his clothes off, and then standing panting, dick hard and pointing straight ahead, and every nerve in his body telling him to take care of Vale, to plug him with his cock, to end his pain.

But…no, first… First, he had to think.

Think, Jason. Think.

Condoms.

He had two. Fuck. Just two. He scraped nails over his scalp, trying to focus over the violent urge in himself to put Vale's suffering to an end. Finally, he caved, falling to his knees behind Vale and covering him with his body from behind.

"I'm here, baby. I'm here."

"Help me. It hurts. Please." The effort it took for Vale to say that alone was evident, and he shook all over, his entire body shaking. It was clear he'd been in pain a long time, too long. Possibly it'd started not long after Jason had left, and he'd been hurting for an hour or more now.

Fuck.

"I've got you. I'm going to help you, Vale. I promise."

He swallowed hard, wishing he had packed an alpha dildo. It wouldn't do the job long term, but it would help. But he had something else. Something that might hold Vale off for a while, long enough to make the condoms last longer than tonight. Maybe.

"Listen, baby. I'm going to need you to relax and let me in."

"Please," Vale whimpered. He shoved his ass back and presented in lordosis position. Jason had done a study on the genetic origins of that position with Dr. Obi before graduating and still found it the most mesmerizing thing in the world. An omega in lordosis presentation was the sexiest thing imaginable. "Knot me. Please."

Jason kissed Vale's heaving rib cage, the muscles and bone showing starkly with each breath. Then he slipped his hand down, pressing three fingers against Vale's hole. It was sopping wet with slick, and he sank in easily. Then he pulled out and added his pinky before withdrawing and curling in his thumb. All four fingers and the widest part of his hand moved inexorably into Vale who held incredibly still, crying out as the swollen slick glands gushed and wetness slipped down his thighs to the carpet beneath his knees.

"That's good," Jason said. "Just let me inside." Carefully, he curled his fingers and made a fist inside Vale's body—a simulacrum of a knot. Vale's muscles released and he collapsed onto the sofa, spasms wracking him as he came. "That's my perfect omega," Jason praised.

Vale trembled and shook on his fist, and Jason pumped it slowly, twisting his wrist, and working over the swollen slick glands. He knew that Vale needed the fullness of his knot and the alpha pheromones released when he knotted, but this could help alleviate the pain of his swollen glands, help him come, and keep him from being in too much pain.

In the meantime, Jason's mind frantically searched for a solution to the condom problem. He considered and discarded each household item and fabric he might fashion into makeshift condoms. There was the aluminum foil that he'd brought. He could wrap it tightly around… But, no, that couldn't be safe. It was metal after all. A rubber glove? He considered whether there might be one or two under the kitchen sink to wear when washing dishes. He'd have to check later.

"Wolf-god, darling," Vale murmured. "Harder. More."

Jason worked his arm in and out, twisting his wrist and angling against the omega glands with his knuckles. Vale's legs trembled and shook, and his anus spasmed along with the muscled depths of his insides. He crooned and cried out, already too far gone to worry about what came next.

No, that was Jason's job as alpha.

He was relieved when the wave passed without needing his knot to drive it away, and he helped Vale up onto the sofa, shaking and disoriented as he was, while he went to wash his hands and check the kitchen for rubber gloves and the thin plastic wrap that could be used to cover sandwiches.

There were neither. He sat at the kitchen table, obscured by a divider from Vale's resting place on the couch, and put his head in his hands. Tears welled in his eyes. He needed to find something— anything to protect Vale. He rose and went down the hall to their luggage, sorting through their clothing, looking for something with a thick enough weave to catch at least some of his semen. But the way alphas unloaded as they knotted, the force, the amount…he knew it wouldn't be enough.

Giving up, he opened the First Aid kit and took out the two condoms inside. He'd delay using them as long as possible. But he knew it was only a matter of time before he had to choose between letting Vale suffer and possibly impregnating him.

He hoped he was strong enough to listen to the screams. He had to be. There was no other choice.

FOUR HOURS LATER, they'd moved into the bedroom for comfort. Jason was exhausted, and Vale was barely satisfied.

Jason's arm muscles ached from pumping his fist in and out of Vale's body, and his unrelieved cock drooled incessantly on the floor. He was aching all over to do what nature intended—impale Vale on his cock, fuck him until they were both wrecked with lust and pleasure, and then knot him as he pumped his cum into Vale's waiting womb.

Speaking of his womb, it had dropped. Jason felt it sucking at his knuckles as he moved his fist up and down in Vale, open and ready for the head of his alpha cock to push inside. Vale shuddered on his wrist, shivering as Jason used his knuckles to tease the mouth of his womb, sending him into tremors and runs of orgasms.

Jason kissed Vale's inner thighs, watching as slick pulsed out around his wrist and soaked into the sheets. The heady scent of slick and Vale's cum rose around them, and he rutted his cock against the mattress, fighting against the urge to withdraw his fist, and replace it with his dick.

Vale was delirious now. He clearly ached with dissatisfaction. So far, Jason's fisting had prevented his screams of pain and agony, but it wasn't going to last. Jason could feel the ramping up of the heat, the unrelieved pressure building as he denied Vale his knot and the pheromones that went with it. He needed to use one of the condoms soon, but he kept holding back, waiting until the pain began again. It wouldn't be long now. He could sense the building need in Vale. And that unsatisfied demand overflowed into seductive, anxious omega bed talk—all inhibitions lost in the drive to get Jason's knot.

"That's it darling," Vale whimpered, green eyes glimmering with arousal. "Feel that?"

Jason kissed Vale's thigh again and nodded.

"Push into me. More. Please."

Jason shoved his fist against the mouth of Vale's womb and moaned as it sucked and grabbed at him. Vale tried to hunch down against Jason's fist, wanting it in deeper, wanting him to penetrate his womb and force more orgasms from him. But Jason knew it would never satisfy him like a knot, and he'd never put his fist in there before. For all he knew, it wasn't safe or might hurt him. He held back.

"Don't you want to fill me up?" Vale asked breathlessly.

Jason gasped. "Yes, yes."

"Show me. Show me how much do you want me. Now."

Jason's cock jerked, and he rubbed his cheek along Vale's thigh, scenting him and holding out against his instincts. "Not yet."

"Now, please Jason, now," Vale pleaded, voice going wobbly and tears filling his eyes. "Please. Please. I need it. I *need* it. It hurts."

Jason bit his cheek and squeezed his eyes closed. He worked his fist into Vale harder and faster, letting out a stream of breath when Vale clenched up around him and came, cursing and sobbing, whimpering and begging Jason for his knot.

"Not enough," Vale said, coming down from the orgasm. "Not enough. Knot me. Please, if you love me at all—"

"Baby, I love you. You're my everything. I have to save the condoms."

"Now, Jason. Now. Oh, fuck, wolf-god, now, now, *now*." Vale's head tossed back and forth on the bed. His asshole went tight around Jason's wrist as sweat poured off him in a fresh wave. He screamed, his muscles going rigid, and Jason cursed, locked inside Vale until this misery passed. He should have gone ahead and knotted him. He should have listened. He'd failed his omega, his *Érosgápe*, his Vale.

Jason murmured and soothed, tears pricking his own eyes as Vale screamed and shook, convulsing in horrific torment on Jason's hand. And then, finally, after far too long and way too much anguish, Vale fell back on the mattress in a swoon, releasing his grip around Jason's arm. Jason slowly, carefully pulled his hand free. A wealth of sweet-smelling slick rushed after it. He sat at the foot of the bed forlornly, watching as Vale's unconscious and now very pale form sucked in harsh, stuttery breaths—his limbs still twitching in pain.

"I'm sorry," Jason whispered, though Vale couldn't hear him.

"I'll give you what you need."

He grabbed the first of the two condoms. He tore open the packet and gasped. The condom inside was dry and flaky. He pulled it free, and it fell apart in his fingers. "No, no, no."

He ripped open the second condom, and horror clogged his throat as it also came apart in his hands. The packages indicated that the condoms were six years old, and the material used wasn't meant to last longer than three. He threw the wrappers across the room, a scream of dread and grief forcing its way from his mouth.

Vale twitched and moaned. Jaw tight, and the hand of fear squeezing his heart, Jason climbed up the bed to lay where Vale could see him when he woke. He stroked Vale's cheek gently, and when *finally* Vale did open his eyes, Jason almost started crying. He had failed his *Érosgápe*. He'd failed Vale. And it hurt so much to witness the wash of relief in Vale's eyes as he saw him.

"Thank wolf-god, Jason," Vale rasped. "I need you. It hurts so much. I can't take it. Help me. Please."

"Shh, baby. You don't have to beg." Jason felt like a liar saying that, though, because he'd already made Vale beg, and then been forced to watch him suffer. To scream and twist in pain—to convulse with agony instead of pleasure. He couldn't take it. He couldn't watch another second of it, couldn't listen to that pain. He was weak. He was too soft for that. "Vale…"

"Jason, please help me."

"Baby, the condoms—"

"I don't care," Vale said. "I don't care anymore. Just please make it stop." His eyes filled with tears. "I can't do it. I'm too old to handle it. I'm scared."

Jason's throat closed. No more. No more of that. He climbed between Vale's legs and positioned his hard, dripping cock. He was too frightened and numb even to feel the pleasure when he first pressed in, though the heat and friction soothed the part of him that needed this, too.

"Ohhhhh, yessssss," Vale hissed as Jason forced his cock past the swollen slick glands and over his prostate. Vale's eyes rolled up, and he smiled in relief as he felt the familiar length and breadth of Jason's cock. His legs trembled around Jason's waist, and his passage rippled with an orgasm. "Darling, yes, oh, thank you. *Thank you.*"

Jason buried his head against Vale's neck, breathing in his scent, tears pricking his eyes. He'd betrayed Vale. He was condomless and on the verge of doing something neither of them had ever wanted, something Vale had almost walked away from their special bond to avoid—he was about to breed his omega.

Jason whimpered, horrified by the smell of Vale's pain laced with need and lust, and when Vale began to twist with the beginnings of pain again, he began to thrust determinedly. Wolf-god, this wasn't how he'd ever dreamed of this moment—raw and sweet inside Vale's heat-open body. But it was the only way. He couldn't let Vale suffer for a moment more.

The heat of Vale's body grew intense, and the grip of his passage so strong and perfect. Friction mounted—his cock massaged by swollen slick glands, and the convulsions of Vale's inner walls as he obtained pleasure after pleasure, orgasms rolling through him with the ease of all omegas in heat. Jason knew he wouldn't be able to last long, either. He didn't even want to. He'd made Vale wait far too long already, let him hurt, and he wasn't going to allow him to ache for a moment more.

"Please! Knot me," Vale groaned, lifting his ass to capture Jason's cock with every desperate thrust. "I want it. I want it *so much*, darling. Please. Oh, *please.*"

The begging was more than Jason could take, and he held Vale's lithe body tight as he rutted into him, fast, hard, delirious, and without any care now except to get his knot.

Vale's wails of pleasure rose around him, and the shudders of his body were all ecstasy and bliss. Jason rode Vale's convulsions easily before shoving deep inside. He yelled as the head of his cock pushed past the clingy, soft mouth of Vale's womb, and the violent understanding that he was flesh-to-flesh, cock-to-womb in Vale's body rocked him to the core. His cockhead massaged by the strong convulsions of Vale's muscled womb, Jason unloaded wad after wad of thick semen with a shout of pleasure.

Vale cried out, too, reaching down to hold Jason's ass and drag him in as deeply as possible. His own orgasms ravaged him—womb and anal and penile all at once. Cum burst from his cock to paint his and Jason's stomachs and chests. All his muscles tensed and released in pulsing rhythm. Vale was wild with pleasure, and he screamed with joy. The delicious burst of Vale's pheromones responding to Jason's knotting scents filled Jason's nose and reassured him that the cries were sheer bliss, not a return of the pain.

Jason's knot grew quickly, locking them together, and he groaned as it filled up Vale's muscled passage. Vale's internal spasms gripped his knot and forced him to release jet after jet of cum right into Vale's fertile womb.

Jason quaked and quivered, losing himself in the perfection of coming inside his *Érosgápe*—of joining himself with Vale, and the knowledge that he was truly, for the first time, naked inside his womb. When Jason came back from that mind-blowing high, reality hit him like a train. The panic of what might happen next replaced the bliss of joining. Trembling overtook him, and he willed his knot to go down so that he could withdraw and wash the semen from Vale's body. But to no avail. They were together until his body let them release, and by then…

Vale's fingers gently stroked his back. Jason stayed buried deep in Vale's womb, feeling the twitching of it around his cockhead, and the trembling of Vale's passage on his knot. He became aware of Vale's stillness beneath him, the realization of what had taken place evident in Vale's slight tension and silence.

"I'm sorry," Jason finally whispered, unable to get enough words around the violent lump in his throat to say more, to explain about the condoms, to beg Vale to forgive him.

"I'm not," Vale murmured. "You feel so beautiful. I never thought I'd feel this—the heat of your cum in my womb, the softness of your flesh in mine."

Jason collapsed against Vale, his knot swollen, and he bit at Vale's shoulders, trying to hold back his tears, but they came anyway. Sobs ripped out of him like torn hunks of his flesh, and each jolt of his heartbreak rubbed his knot inside Vale's sensitive body and sent him into spasms of pleasure.

Beneath him, breathless and shaking, Vale wrapped his arms around Jason, brushing soothing strokes down his back. "Baby alpha, you have to be strong for me. We have *days* of this left."

Jason nodded against Vale's shoulder, tears still leaking from his eyes as he lifted up and peered down into Vale's face. "I have you, Vale. Don't be scared."

Vale touched his face, wiping the tears off his cheek. "Yes, you've got me. And I'm not scared, I promise." He smiled sweetly. "I'm with you."

Jason broke down again, his sobs once again sending Vale into a frenzy of physical pleasure. "Oh, wolf-god, Jason, I can't stop. I'm sorry. Just…oh, oooohhhh."

It took long minutes before Jason could get his heart in enough check that Vale could finally calm on his knot again. Eyes glassy with pleasure and exhaustion, Vale gazed up at him when the sobs receded. He reached up and wiped at the tears leaking down Jason's face. "Don't cry, darling. What's done is done. Let's enjoy this since we can't stop it."

Jason nodded, determined not to burden Vale with his hideous guilt. "I love you."

"I'm not scared, Jason. Do you feel how good we are?" Vale murmured, tensing slightly beneath Jason. "You deep in my womb. Me receiving you. The beginning and the end."

"Not the end," Jason gritted out, shaking his head.

Vale's shiny eyes softened. "No, darling. Not the end."

Jason smiled down at him, trying to be strong like Vale asked. Yet he couldn't stop crying entirely until his knot had softened. As he carefully pulled out, appalled to see the huge gush of semen from Vale's gaping hole, he swallowed back the last of his tears and carefully inserted his fingers in Vale to help ease him down until the next wave hit.

"I love you. And I'm not scared either." Jason's voice trembled.

Vale laughed, and that sweet, familiar sound held all the fear that had gripped both of their hearts. "Of course, you're not." He smiled wryly, obviously humoring Jason. "You're my strong, fearless alpha. My everything."

"And you're my everything," Jason whispered in reply.

The words hung between them, huge and true, and Jason didn't know how he was going to live without Vale if he fell pregnant from this heat. His mind went to Urho and his handling of unwanted pregnancies for omegas, and Jason's pater who had connections with the pharmacist in the Calitan district. There were other options no matter what happened. Scary options, but they'd get through them together.

They had to.

Suddenly Vale groaned, and squirmed beneath him, "Oh, *fuck*. Here it comes again." He gripped Jason's chin and said desperately. "Please, Jason, relish it. Take my body and enjoy it. Don't taint this beautiful thing we're sharing with fear for a future outcome that might not even happen."

Jason kissed his collarbones and his throat and his jaw. Vale was right. There was no guarantee that he would fall pregnant. He was, after all, a bit older than most, and these unexpected heats were often a sign of decreased fertility. It might be that he was scared for nothing. He should take Vale's advice. Feel this beautiful union fully. Revel in it because they might never get to experience it again for a lot of reasons.

Vale arched. "Oh, it's back. Wolf-god, darling, please. Make me come again."

So, Jason, terrified and more in love than ever, did.

PART TWO

CITY PREGNANCY

CHAPTER FOUR

D R. URHO CHASE was being his usual uptight, rigid self, and really, Jason had no idea how Vale had ever let the man fuck him for fun, much less handle his heats. Jason's jaw clenched hard. Now wasn't the time to think about that. Jason was fragile at the moment—scared and hurt. Alpha expression fairly lived beneath his skin, just looking for a reason to lash out.

Vale sat in the wing-backed chair in his study, the one he and Jason had first fucked in, sealing their bond, and breaking all the protocols of the time. Fucking like that without a contract had been reckless. He'd been reckless, and it seemed he still was. A clear pattern was establishing itself in their lives together. He didn't deserve Vale as his omega, his beloved.

"Jason," Vale said sharply. "Please stop pacing. You're making me feel sick."

Instantly, Jason stopped and dropped to his knees by Vale's side. He took Vale's hand and asked, "Do you want some fizzy water? I'll get it for you. With lemon?"

"No. I want you to be still." Vale's fingers sank into Jason's hair, and he combed through it soothingly as he eyed Urho where he waited, obviously anxious underneath his condescending attitude. "So, that's where we stand," Vale went on, having been the one to tell Urho everything about their trip, his unexpected heat, and the apparent consequences because Jason was too horrified and overcome to talk about it even now. "What are our options?"

Urho took a deep breath, and his nose twitched.

"You smell it, too?" Vale asked. "Jason scented a change in me almost immediately after the heat."

Jason trembled and pressed his face to Vale's knee. He'd nearly lost his mind the final night in the cabin when he realized that the odd scent he kept picking up over dinner was coming from Vale. The scent of a growing baby. Their baby.

"You should have called me as soon as you got back," Urho said quietly. "The herbal remedies often work in the earliest stages."

"I didn't see any reason to think that I could be pregnant," Vale said, putting his chin out. "No reason to endure cramping and bleeding if there was no babe."

"No reason to…" Urho huffed dramatically and spread his hands wide, snarling. "This boy pumped loads of his cum in your fertile womb for four days straight, and you didn't think there was any reason to think you might be pregnant?" He scoffed. "Irresponsible. Both of you. Especially you, Jason. You call yourself an alpha?"

Jason growled but then whimpered. He hung his head, shame filling him from foot to crown.

Vale snapped. "Don't do that to him. He's already tearing himself up over this. He did what any alpha would do."

Urho raised a skeptical brow that made Jason want to punch him but only after eviscerating himself first. Hissing, he said, "He entered you, left his cum in you, all while knowing the consequences of a pregnancy."

"Urho," Vale bit out. "We're *Érosgápe*. Tell me you could have let Riki suffer. Tell me you could have sat there by his bed and listened as he howled in pain. When he was dying, did you regret that you'd—"

Urho cracked. "Wolf-god! Don't speak of that."

"Tell me you would have done it differently."

Urho's shoulders sank. "I couldn't have. Never." He turned to

Jason then and said in a gentler tone, "You did what you were supposed to do."

Jason shook his head, his throat tight. "I killed him."

"No. You fucked him, which is what our very natures demand. Why do you think omegas suffer so much?"

Jason cast his mind back to Alpha-Omega Relations class and whispered, "Because their glands become inflamed, and their nerves are—"

"Not medically, but evolutionarily," Urho interrupted, his voice gruff. "Their agony calls to us. It breaks down any reluctance on our part to knot and breed. Their pain is so great that it *forces* us to soothe them. It is wolf-god's plan."

Jason scoffed at the idea of a god who would use agony as a motivator. What kind of god was that?

Stepping closer to them, Urho reached down to squeeze Jason's shoulder. "It's hard enough to stand by when any omega is hurting in heat. An *Érosgápe*? Impossible. Don't beat yourself up about this."

Jason gritted his teeth and said nothing, pulling away from Urho's attempt at fatherly comfort. He hated him for his condescension. Hated him for acting like Jason had done anything other than let Vale down in every way possible. He knew that if he'd never entered Vale's life, then Urho would have continued to handle Vale's heats, and none of this would have ever happened. Vale would be safe, and—

He twitched.

And Urho's. And that wasn't possible. Every cell in his body rebelled at that, and he snarled at Urho, held back only by Vale's hand circling his wrist.

"It's not Urho's fault that he's an asshole," Vale said softly. "He's given his best version of an apology. Accept it and let's move on to the part where he explains what we can still try."

Urho sighed and turned to his black medical bag. "I should examine you, confirm the pregnancy, but I don't trust that it's a good idea right now." He gave Jason a pointed look. "We both scent it on you. It seems well-latched given the intensity of the change in your smell, and yet the place to start is still with the herbs." He opened the bag and withdrew a few tins, sorting through the pills inside, and creating a special assortment in an empty tin for Vale. "Plus a few stronger abortifacients. Less legal ones."

These he handed to Jason, who took them and stared at the skull and crossbones label on the side. "This is poison?"

"Of course. That's what kills the babe, makes it unlatch, and creates the cramping to expel him. At this stage, it's unlikely to be dangerous. It will make Vale sick as a dog, but it isn't enough to hurt him, of course."

Kills the babe.

Jason shuddered at the brutal words. He swallowed hard. He couldn't admit it, not to Vale, not to anyone, but the scent of Vale and the baby combined was far from repugnant. It was divine. Delicious. The most perfect scent he'd ever caught except for Vale's when Jason had imprinted on him in the library. Viscerally, he wanted it to grow stronger, to expand and fill the house, and the idea of ending it, cutting it short…

He swallowed the thick lump in his throat again. Fuck. There was no good solution. Nothing painless. Everything hurt.

Vale had placed a hand on his stomach, his skin looking paler than usual, and his pulse thrumming in his neck. "Kill the babe," he whispered, clearly caught on the same words that had pierced Jason in the heart.

"Vale," Urho said, his voice hitching sadly, "there's no other way."

Vale reached for the tin in Jason's hands, looked at it, and squeezed his eyes shut. "I take these all at once, or…?"

"All at once. Then make yourself as comfortable as possible. The pain will be intense when the cramps take over, but nothing as bad as an unserviced heat. Your memories of that must be bright enough still. This will pale in comparison."

"I...don't..." Vale stared at the tin some more, the silver glinting in the light from the windows. "I'm cold."

Jason moved dully but immediately to the fireplace. Laying the fire was easy enough, but it felt good to take even a small action that went toward caring for Vale. He'd done everything he could since they'd returned from the trip to make it up to Vale, to show him he was sorry that he hadn't been stronger. But Vale didn't seem to understand what he was doing, taking his service to him as evidence of his fear alone, and lost in his own thoughts about what might be coming.

Or, once Vale took the pills in that tin, wouldn't be coming.

"Jason?" Urho asked. "Did you hear me? You will need to keep him under observation, and if there is excessive bleeding like what you witnessed with your pater, then you must call an ambulance to come. If there are questions, you'll say it was a miscarriage. You'll both look miserable enough that they'll believe you. This once anyway. But you won't be making a habit of it."

The reference to Jason's pater's losses was also horrible, and Jason rubbed a hand over his eyes, trying to block out the horrifying memory of his beloved pater on his knees, bleeding profusely and crying in pain. He wouldn't be able to stand seeing Vale like that.

"Urho, really, you are too blunt today," Vale scolded. "He's scared, can't you see that?" He reached out his hand for Jason to come to him, but Jason didn't.

Jason straightened his shoulders instead and said, "We're all scared, Vale. You don't need to tiptoe around me."

Vale's brows quirked, and so did his mouth, but he didn't argue, which was kind of him. Jason knew he'd been less than what

Vale needed since they got back. Not nearly stoic enough. Crazy with worry. Compulsive in his care.

"Please leave us," Vale said to quietly to Urho. "Thank you for coming. You've been the best friend to us both, and I love you for it."

Jason bristled slightly, but let it roll off. It wasn't that kind of love for Vale. It never had been. For Urho, however? Yes. He'd loved Vale—and probably still did—with the kind of romantic ardor that Vale deserved, and which Jason worked hard to ignore. Because otherwise he'd have to murder Urho, and that seemed like the sort of thing Vale would have a hard time forgiving him for. And the sort of thing he'd have a hard time forgiving himself for, too. Consciences were a pain in the ass.

Urho issued some further instructions regarding the pills and Jason heard them through a wall of white noise. Watch Vale's temperature. Keep him cool. Let him cramp and bleed and pass the child out of his body. "Don't be surprised if he comes out in more than one piece," Urho said calmly in the same way Jason might say, "Don't be surprised if the daffodil bulbs multiply."

Vale made a choking noise at that and Jason hustled to his side, dropped to his knees, and wrapped his arms around Vale's middle. He said nothing, though, holding Vale hard but not talking, because what could he possibly say? They were going to destroy the most beautiful thing they'd ever made.

"Call me if you need help," Urho said, putting his hand on Jason's head in a way that should have pissed him off, but instead felt like sympathy and shared sadness. "You know my number."

Then Urho left them alone with the tin of pills and the silence of the study.

"Mreow." The small noise came from beneath the sofa, and Zephyr crept out, her silver fur gleaming in the morning light from the windows. She bounded onto the hearth and perched there, watching them with her golden eyes, still as a statue.

"I wonder if he would have your eyes," Vale whispered, and Jason held him even closer, pressing his face to Vale's stomach and scenting the small seed of their child growing in there. "Your hair."

They were silent for a long moment until Zephyr broke her pose and trotted through the door into the hallway.

"I wanted children," Vale said. "My whole life, I wanted them."

"Vale," Jason said cautiously. "Don't do this to yourself."

"I want this child, Jason."

Jason swallowed, and tears filled his eyes. He sat back on his heels. "I know. But you can't have him."

Vale pressed his lips into a grim line, and he clenched the tin convulsively. "I could."

"No."

"I don't have to take these."

"Vale, baby, you can't leave me." Jason's voice broke. "Please. I know this is hard. I want him, too. I can smell how perfect and beautiful he is, and I know that he's part of you, and part of me, and...fuck..." He broke off, the tears that kept coming ever since the heat in the mountain cabin overwhelmed him again. "I want him, too, but we can't have him. We can't."

Vale sat very still. His knuckles white around the tin. "You want him, too?"

Ice dripped into Jason's veins. His eyes went wide. "Whatever your thinking, don't. Don't do this to me."

Vale nodded slowly. "You're right. I know you're right."

Jason took him by the hand and pulled him up from the wingback chair. "Let's get it over with, baby. Before we second-guess ourselves."

Before you make me lose you entirely.

IN THE BATHROOM, standing in front of the mirror, Vale held the small white pills in his hand. He could hear Jason in their bedroom, readying the bed with old towels to catch the blood and gore should the pills work. Vale shuddered and put his hand over his stomach.

He was naked now. Jason had helped him out of his soft pants and t-shirt, kissing his shoulders, pecs, and thighs as he did. There'd been nothing sensual in it. No, it'd been worshipful, sorrowful, and scared. Like he needed Vale to understand that every part of him was what Jason needed—now and always.

I want him, too.

Vale heard the words again. Jason's voice had trembled and shaken with grief as he'd spit the confession out. His alpha wanted their child—probably just as much as Vale did, if not more. And the one thing Vale had been afraid of from the start had come to pass. He was denying Jason a family. His injuries and scars were depriving the best man in the world—the sweetest alpha to ever live, the most beautiful soul he'd ever know, the most loving boy in the whole world—a family of his own.

What would happen if he didn't end it? What other options were there? The last time he'd gone to Urho for a checkup, he'd asked him to check the scar tissue. But he'd noticed it wasn't as painful when he and Jason had sex now, and that it seemed to be more amenable to rough activities like fisting. Which Jason loved to do, and Vale enjoyed as well. Riding Jason's wrist with his fist balled up inside him as a makeshift knot was always beautiful between heats. During heat, it wasn't enough, but for the months in between…perfect.

Urho had said the scar tissue did seem more elastic, and he credited Jason's persistent use of Vale's body for stretching it out and breaking down the inelasticity of the tissue. He'd also mentioned the natural properties of alpha sperm for reducing the residual inflammation. That had been months ago. Would it be even softer now?

"Vale?" Jason called from the bedroom.

"Be right out."

"Are you taking them now?"

Vale stared at the white pills, so stark against the flesh of his palm. A strange sense of unreality gripped him, and almost like he was in a dream, he tipped his hand so the pills fell in the toilet.

"No," he said firmly. "I'm not."

Then he flushed them away.

CHAPTER FIVE

VALE WAS CERTAIN Jason was going to have a heart attack if he didn't calm down, and yet his baby alpha was so upset that Vale didn't dare get close for fear he'd accidentally get in the way of Jason's flailing arms.

"How could you do this? How? I'm calling Urho. I'm calling him now."

"What good will that do, darling?" Vale asked quietly. "I'm not taking the pills."

He sat on their big bed, back to the headboard and naked from the waist up. He'd pulled his soft pants on again but left the t-shirt where Jason had let it fall to the floor earlier. He held a pillow over his chest and stomach, clutching it for comfort as Jason madly paced the bedroom floor.

"You will take them," Jason said, pointing a long finger at him. Oh, how Vale loved those fingers. So beautifully formed and so generous when on his body. "You will take them, or I'll force you to take them."

Vale pressed his lips together, saying nothing. He waited for Jason to hear his words for himself. Which, of course, he did after only a moment.

"Please, Vale. Don't do this. I'm sorry. I know I can't make you take them, but wolf-god, please—for me, for our love, for our life together—please take them. Please."

"I flushed them," Vale reminded him. "I don't have any to take. And I won't take them, even if you have Urho bring more."

"Could he talk sense into you?" Jason asked angrily, throwing his arms wide. "If he came over, could he get it into your head that you cannot, must not, *will not* have this baby?"

"You want him, too," Vale whispered.

Jason's mouth worked, and tears flooded his eyes. "Not at this cost!"

"We don't know that it will cost my life."

"We do! We've always known that. It will cost your life. I'll lose you. I'll be alone and without you. Forever." His voice broke, his eyes growing desperate. "Don't do that to me. Don't leave me alone here."

Vale opened his arms wide, inviting Jason into them, but Jason kept his distance, staring at Vale with such seething hurt that Vale felt it in his own chest. "Baby alpha, listen to me. We'll call Urho tomorrow. Have him look me over, check the scar tissue again, and see—"

"I don't want his fingers in your body."

"I know you don't, but he's a doctor, and he will be honest. If it's not any better, if there's not an improvement to the elasticity, then I'll take the pills tomorrow."

Jason gazed at him. A shiver passed over his body. "Don't lie to me."

Vale swallowed hard. "I want your child. Our child. Please let me try."

"No."

"It's my body."

"You're mine. My *Érosgápe*. My omega. You may not have this baby. I won't allow it."

Vale let loose a small, sad sound. "Oh, sweet baby boy, come here." Jason took an involuntary step forward and then stopped dead.

"No. You won't have him."

"You can't stop me from trying."

"I order you to stop this nonsense, Vale. Stop it. Now. Stop it!"

Vale rubbed a hand over his face. "I love you. More than my own life."

Jason's lips quivered, his face splotched with fury. "I don't want you to do this for me. I don't want this baby."

"But Jason, you do."

Vale held himself firm as Jason crumpled to the floor, curling in on himself, and begging with every breath. Finally, Vale slowly rose from the bed and crouched down beside Jason on the floor, wrapped his arms around him and murmured, "This isn't your choice. It's mine."

JASON HAD NEVER thought himself capable of hating Vale, but as he stood beside him inside Urho's clinic, he thought he might. He felt so helpless and betrayed, but Vale was calm. Deadly calm. Stubborn as hell. Mind made up. He'd only seen him like this one other time, and he'd nearly lost him then.

He wasn't going to lose him now.

"Just make him take the pills," Jason gritted out when Urho stood gaping at Vale like an especially handsome fish. "Or inject him. Please. Urho. Help me."

Vale shot him a dark glance but kept his mouth shut otherwise, and Urho ignored Jason like he didn't even exist.

"You want me to examine you? Vale, we've been over this—"

"No, that was years ago. At my last checkup, you said the scar tissue was—"

"He had his fingers in you? When!" Jason placed himself in between Urho and Vale, anger and fear making a muddle of all his protective instincts. "You've touched him?"

Urho scoffed and shoved Jason aside. Jason had grown a lot over the last few years and was more a man than ever, but Urho was muscled, and he could still move Jason like he was a dumb, teenaged pup. "I'm a doctor. Get over yourself. Good alphas don't prevent their omegas from receiving medical care."

Jason huffed and lunged at Urho, but Vale cried out. "Enough!"

It took everything Jason had to let go of Urho's shirt.

Urho dusted himself off, gave Jason a disdainful look, and then said, "If you want to stay in here for the examination, you will get your act together, and you will not touch me again."

Jason felt dizzy. The idea of being expelled from this room while Urho touched his pregnant omega, put his fingers in his body…

"I'll stay," he gritted out.

"Jason," Vale said sharply. "I understand that you're scared and angry, but you will *not* hurt him or interfere in this examination, do you understand me? Or there will be consequences. You won't like those."

Jason wasn't sure Vale had ever spoken to him in that way, and he jerked as if slapped. The sting of Vale's tone brought him up short, and he nodded. "I understand."

Vale sighed, rubbing a hand over his beard. "You said that there was elasticity now that wasn't there before. Remember?"

"Not enough to grow a child, Vale," Urho said gently with that emotional tenderness he reserved for Vale alone. Jason hated him. Hated this entire moment and hated himself for being such an uncontrolled baby alpha that he'd been unable to prevent himself from impregnating Vale to begin with.

"Just…check again. I used to feel it on Jason's knot. But this last heat…" Vale shook his head. "Nothing. Not on his fist. Not on his knot. The scars didn't hurt at all."

Urho gave Jason a dark look. "Behave yourself." To Vale, he

said, "Undress and climb on the examining table. I'll be back in a moment." Then he went out the door.

Jason stood in a corner, shamed and angry, watching Vale take his clothes off and slip on a hospital gown. He left it open in the front, which made Jason nearly vibrate with irritation, but he held himself back. If he hadn't been able to control himself during the heat, he'd control himself entirely now. His breath came in and out in fast, obnoxious gulps.

Vale settled himself on the examining table and then reached out to Jason, silently asking for his hand. Jason relented and came to stand by the table, his eyes aching from the tears and lack of sleep the last few nights. Everything seemed to shift and tremble around him as if he were in a dream state and not reality.

"It's all right," Vale soothed. "Urho is going to check me. Don't get possessive. I'm all yours."

Jason bent to nuzzle at Vale's beard, loving the soft scratch against his cheek. Vale stoked the back of his neck reassuringly.

A single knock preceded the door cracking open. "Are we ready?" Urho asked gruffly.

"Yes," Vale affirmed.

He entered with a small beta nurse by his side. The man nodded brusquely at Jason, acknowledging him as an alpha, and then stood off where he wouldn't see any intimate parts of Vale's body while Urho did his check.

"This is Henny," Urho said. "He's my nurse, and he'll be here help out."

Vale nodded, clearly accustomed to a beta nurse being in the room for a checkup. Jason frowned, not thrilled with yet another person witnessing Vale in a vulnerable state, but he kept his mouth clamped shut. Despite Vale being tender with him and asking for his hand, he suspected that he was on the verge of being on Vale's shit list right now. Not for his lack of control during the heat, but for his utter and complete panic the last few days. He knew it was his job as alpha to support Vale, to keep him calm and safe. But his stubborn omega was making him crazy by even entertaining the idea of having the baby. Nothing was worth losing Vale. Not even the temptation of a child.

"Lean back." Urho gave Jason another glower. "Should he stay or go?"

"Jason will be calm," Vale said, and it was an order, not a request.

Jason nodded and took Vale's hand again as he settled on his back, his feet propped up on the table. Vale spread his knees wide, revealing everything beneath his hospital gown to Urho. Jason gritted his teeth and watched as Urho pulled on a medical glove, added a touch of lube to his fingers, and then pressed his hand between Vale's thighs.

Vale's breath hitched, and Jason barely held back his growl. But then Vale relaxed, his eyes fixed on the ceiling.

Henny, the beta nurse, stayed where he was by the wall, simply observing the scene while respecting Vale's privacy as much as possible. Urho frowned, shoved his hand more firmly, and Vale squeaked slightly. Jason gripped his hand tighter, more to keep himself from punching Urho than to reassure Vale.

"Feel that?" Urho asked.

Vale said, "Yes."

"That's still a bit tight."

"But less tight?"

Urho sighed and said nothing, moving his arm around, and feeling up inside Vale. "This doesn't hurt? When I push here?"

"No," Vale said quietly. "It's not entirely comfortable. But it doesn't hurt."

"Hmm."

Urho didn't withdraw his hand, and Henny stepped up closer,

obviously curious now.

"Before, there was some scar tissue," Urho said to him, explaining. "Dangerously tight flesh that would not have expanded with a pregnancy."

"And now?" the nurse asked.

Urho's brows drew lower, and he moved his hand inside Vale again. Jason shifted so he could see where his hand entered him and then had to step back quickly. The sight of another alpha penetrating his *Érosgápe* was absolutely maddening, even though, logically, he knew it was a medical examination only.

"There seems to be more flexibility than before. It's still tight, but there's a good deal of release when I press against the flesh." He checked Vale's face. "Truly. Be honest. That doesn't hurt? Don't be stubborn, Vale."

"I told you, it's not comfortable, but it doesn't hurt."

Urho sighed and withdrew his hand slowly, and Vale let out a soft sound that made Jason's knees a little weak. Vale squeezed Jason's hand again as though to reassure him, and Jason gave a tense, closed-lipped smile in return.

Urho removed his gloves and moved up then, spreading open Vale's gown and revealing his cock, balls, and stomach. Henny turned away, suddenly busy with organizing a drawer in the corner. Jason held his breath as Urho pressed around on Vale's stomach, his eyes on Vale's face, gauging reactions.

"It's possible…" Urho said, and then his eyes cut to Henny. "You can leave us now. The exam is finished."

Henny nodded politely to Jason and Vale, and then exited the room. Vale sat up and adjusted the gown so that he was completely covered. As soon as he was decent, he put his hand out for Jason to take again and tugged him to stand very close to the exam table where he sat.

"So?" Vale asked.

Urho sighed and sat down in a small chair that he pulled from the corner. He rubbed at his forehead and didn't meet Vale's eyes, his lips pursed in thought.

"Urho," Jason said. "What did you find?"

"The scar tissue is definitely looser now. There is give and stretch that wasn't there before. This is personal, and I apologize in advance," he said, with an eye toward Jason, "but have you been stretching it?"

"Jason likes to fist me," Vale said. "It used to ache and hurt—shh, in an enjoyable way," he said, forestalling Jason's worry on that front, "but lately it hasn't hurt at all, even when he pumps his hand hard."

Urho's face was quite red now and so was Jason's if the burning in his cheeks was any indication. "I see. That's interesting." He furrowed his brow and tapped his chin, finally saying, "During heats, would you say that Jason knots you for longer than former partners?"

Jason shifted from one foot to the other, determined to stay in control, but feeling incredibly irritated to have the image of other alphas sharing knots with Vale pushed into his mind. Especially of Urho himself.

"Definitely. I assumed it was his youth and our *Érosgápe* connection that caused it. At the height of a heat, the knot can last well over an hour."

Urho nodded again. "Well, we know that Alpha semen has anti-inflammatory properties, and some researchers speculate that there are other agents in the semen, too. The building blocks of humanity, certainly, and therefore, perhaps healing properties. We don't need to get into further details, but it seems clear to me that between the stretching from Jason's knot and fist, as well as his semen acting on your old injuries, your scar tissue has changed, relaxed. It's less likely to tear from the weight of a growing child. If labor were induced strategically before the child is at full weight, but still viable, then it's possible you could survive the birth as well." He sounded hesitant, unsure.

"But…?" Jason prompted.

"But I can't guarantee any outcomes. Not yet. I'd want to continue to check you internally as you grow and change. I'd want to monitor this pregnancy closely."

"Of course," Vale said, stunned happiness in his tone. "Are you saying that I don't need to abort? That I can have this child? That *we* can?" He looked up at Jason, his eyes shining, and a bright smile in his dark beard.

Jason's heart caught along with his breath, and he touched Vale's chin lightly, stroking his thumb over the softness of his beard. He didn't want to hear what Urho said next. No answer that would make him happy. Vale, though…Vale seemed ready to celebrate.

"I believe it's possible," Urho agreed. "I underestimated the value of regular internal stretching. I apologize. I should have prescribed regular use of alpha dildos to stretch the scars."

"I think the semen is key," Vale murmured softly. "Daily exposure."

"Sometimes two or three times a day," Jason offered, a stupid surge of pride within, and wanting Urho to know how often he pleasured Vale. And then he felt stupid and young all over again because all it took was one word from Urho to sum it up.

"Teenagers."

Vale rolled his eyes. "Jason's been out of his teens for several years now. I'm just saying that in the past, I could have used alpha dildos to attempt to stretch the scar tissue, but I think the semen has played a role in making it receptive to being stretched."

"Possible," Urho agreed.

"Jason," Vale said, turning to him and offering a shy smile. "Do you know what this means?"

Jason clenched his jaw. He knew exactly what it meant. Vale was going to try to do this. Outcome and risks be damned. "Yes."

"Jason…" He shot a glance toward Urho who rose and left the room with the polite excuse that he would be right back. As soon as Urho shut the door, Vale grabbed Jason's hand hard. "Jason, it means that you're going to be a father."

Jason's throat worked. He tried not to cry again because Vale had to be tired of that. He needed to be a strong alpha. A man. "Does it?" he croaked.

"Yes, and I…" Vale broke into a smile that cut Jason to the quick. "I'm going to be a pater."

CHAPTER SIX

"J ASON, YOU'RE BEING very dramatic," Miner Hoff said, fiddling with the toothpick he tended to keep in his mouth since he'd given up smoking.

Vale almost laughed at that but managed to hold it back, not wanting to hurt his baby alpha any more deeply than he was already hurting.

Jason gaped at his pater, seemingly unable to understand his words, much less his feelings.

When they'd arrived at the Sabel-Hoff house, Jason's pater, Miner—sensing something was deeply wrong—had hustled them both back to his conservatory and plied them with tea and questions. Jason had spilled immediately, even though his father, Yule wasn't home yet. He obviously believed that Miner would immediately take his side after all he'd been through himself with dangerous pregnancies.

"Dramatic?" Jason asked coolly—a tone Vale had never heard him use with anyone, much less either of his much-beloved parents.

"If Vale believes, and the *doctor* believes that he should try—"

"There was no *should!*" Jason exclaimed, pacing in front of the sofa, his shoes clacking on the wooden floor. Music, mainly consisting of horns and brass instruments, played from the record player in the corner. Vale thought he'd always associate this rolling, nauseous feeling with the sound of jazz now. "Urho said he thought it possible Vale could carry nearly to term and deliver safely. *Possible*, Pater. Not likely. Not definitely. There was no certainty involved in his predictions, and definitely no *should!*"

Turning to Vale, Miner's hazel eyes shown with bright interest. "Possible? Truly? That's wonderful. And you want to pursue it?"

"Of course, I want to pursue this baby," Vale said quietly. "More than anything."

Jason threw up his hands. "Where is Father? He'll talk sense into you both."

Miner snorted as he lifted his tea, saying under his breath, "Oh, I highly doubt that."

Vale tended to agree, but he didn't say more. He found that as the days after the heat had passed, he'd tended toward depression. But now, with Urho's assurances, he felt a lightness he couldn't describe. A surety he didn't share with Jason. He needed to find a way to calm his alpha, but he couldn't seem to reach him. Jason was too lost in fear.

Jason continued to pace and curse under his breath as Miner peppered Vale with light, unobtrusive questions that cut to the heart of the matter.

"So, you love him already?" Miner whispered, trying to pitch his voice low so that Jason might not hear, but unable to contain the bubble of excitement the news had blown up in him.

"Yes," Vale agreed. "It's so strange. I don't even know him at all, don't even know if he's an alpha, beta, or omega. But I know he's perfect."

"Of course, he is."

"Like Jason."

"Just so," Miner agreed, casting a loving gaze on his incredibly agitated son. "Though, I doubt he'll look that much like him. He'll likely have your dark hair, certainly. Most pairings with similar coloring to the two of you go that direction. But, with your green eyes, I suppose we could hope for blue like Jason's and Yule's."

"Stop," Jason ordered, his hands raised in front of him. "You're both investing your heart in fairytale dreams. And they won't—*can't* come true. It's not worth the risk."

"What isn't?" Yule asked, stepping into the room with a kiss for his omega and a furrowed brow for Jason. "What's the problem, son, so big that I needed to rush home?"

Jason gestured at his pater and Vale, his cheeks flushed, and his sleepless eyes red. "They're the problem. You need to talk to them. Make them see."

"Really, Jason," his pater said softly. "It's up to Vale. It's his choice."

"No!" Jason exploded. "You know wolf-goddamn well that I'm the one who will suffer." He threw his hands in the air again. "Why did I think you'd be on my side? You tried to do the same thing to Father!"

Miner winced, and Vale put his hand on his pater-in-law's knee, offering a gentle, sympathetic squeeze.

Yule's eyes zeroed in on his *Érosgápe* and then darted back to his son. He stalked to the liquor cabinet and poured a drink for himself. Sipped it, and then, on second thought poured another and brought it over to Jason, pressing it into his hands. "I think you need this. Drink it up while I find out what's happening." He turned his intelligent gaze on Vale then and lifted his brows. "Well?"

"I'm pregnant," Vale said softly. "And the doctor thinks it's possible I can carry him to term."

"Possible," Jason repeated with despair.

His father nudged his arm and indicated the drink. "Finish it."

Jason returned to sipping the dark liquor, most likely brandy, and Yule guided him into one of the chairs by the coffee table Miner had tried to get him to sit in earlier. Then Yule sat down opposite, and they all looked at each other. Eyes darted face to face to face, and around again.

"You're pregnant," Yule said slowly. "How?"

"The usual way." Vale couldn't resist the retort. He wasn't a child, and he didn't like the slightly scolding tone in Yule's voice. The man was barely older than he was.

Yule rolled his eyes. "You know wolf-damned well what I meant by that. Why weren't precautions taken?"

"I'm coming up on forty now," Vale said, sipping the tea that had grown cold as they'd waited for Yule to arrive. "My heats aren't as predictable as they used to be."

Yule flashed a glance toward Miner, a look exchanged, and Vale was quite sure Miner had endured at least one surprise heat before Urho had removed his womb in emergency surgery after his last miscarriage. "I see. There are such things as markets, though. Phones. Someone could have called for a condom delivery to the house before the heat became unbearable. Though why you don't have condoms in your home at all times at your age, I don't know. Or was Jason unable to control himself?"

Jason let out a little hurt sound and Vale took his hand. He was, admittedly, a bit tired of soothing Jason, and wished that he would get on board with Vale's decision and begin offering up the alpha care and attention that a pregnant omega deserved, but he knew Jason was still in shock. He needed some time yet.

"We were at my parents' chalet in the mountains," Vale said since Jason seemed unable to talk.

"The snowstorm," Yule said darkly. "I see."

"The phones were out," Jason said.

Vale felt Jason's guilt eating away at him, and he was going to have to take him to task for that. But not here. Not in front of his parents.

"The doctor says that my scar tissue has healed beyond his expectations," Vale went on. "He believes it's possible—"

"There's that word again!" Jason shouted, standing up to start pacing. "Possible! Vale, that's not enough. I need you. I can't live without you."

Vale rose then, setting his teacup aside, and went to Jason, putting his arms around him. "I know you think that, but alphas do it all the time. Urho, for example, lost his *Érosgápe*, Riki, and he still lives—"

"Like a shadow of a human being!"

"Forget I mentioned him. I shouldn't even let you entertain these thoughts," Vale said with as much calm understanding in his voice that he could summon. "Because I'm not going to die."

"You don't know that."

"Urho would never let me—"

"Urho, Urho, Urho!" Jason slammed back the rest of his drink, dropped the glass onto the mantle by the fireplace, and stalked out of the room.

Vale started to follow him, but Yule held out a hand. "Let me have a minute with him. I understand better than either of you what he's feeling right now."

"I won't change my mind," Vale said firmly.

Yule rolled his eyes. "Of course, you won't."

"So, if you plan to plot with Jason on how to—"

"Vale," Yule said, putting his hands on his hips and heaving a sigh. "I'm not fool enough to think I can change your mind when I couldn't change my own *Érosgápe's* when it mattered most. Jason will come around. And as for me, I would love to be made a grandfather. I've wanted nothing more—you know that. But I also understand his fear of your loss. No pregnancy is safe for an omega, and we heard far too much about your own inability to bear children safely during contract negotiations for me to be entirely easy about it. But since you're determined to see it through…I'll stay positive. And pleased. You'll make a good pater."

Then he turned on his heel and followed his son upstairs. Vale's heart clenched thinking of his baby alpha up on the slanted roof outside his old bedroom window—because of course, that was where he'd gone—probably crying, hurting, and scared.

Miner touched the sofa. "Sit closer to me."

Vale did.

"You promise that Dr. Chase is optimistic?" Miner knew Urho well after his own reproductive emergency had led to Urho attending him.

"He says it's possible," Vale said, rubbing a hand over his beard and wishing desperately that he, too, could have some brandy. But the handouts Urho had given him as they'd left the clinic said that drinking wasn't good for the baby. So, he abstained.

Miner's hazel eyes shaded darker. "Poor Jason's terrified. I hate to see him hurting."

"Me too."

"I know." Miner sighed. "This is always frightening for them. Alphas, I mean. At least, I assume so, based on what my friends have told me of their pregnancies." He chuckled bitterly. "I admit that I never had an easy pregnancy, and Yule was terrified throughout most of them, and, of course, only Jason survived."

"Yes." Vale had always felt sadness for Miner on this front. Of course, he had. But now that he housed so much hope within, he felt for the man deeply, and he was surprised to feel the prick of tears in his eyes. He didn't cry easily—Jason was much more prone to emotional tears, alpha status be damned—but the thought of losing their baby was too much. To think of suffering it again and again as Yule and Miner had done? It was far too much.

Miner shook off the sadness and smiled again. "But yes, my friends tell me their alphas are usually scared, too. Especially at the end, when they are big with child, and so much can go wrong. Even those who aren't *Érosgápe* can get wrapped up in fear."

Vale swallowed hard. Being big with child was something he

hadn't allowed himself to imagine ever being, not since the devastating heat when he was young, the one that had led to the illegal abortion that had left the scars. He'd never believed it possible for him.

"But let's not dwell on the negative," Miner said, quickly. "We have to assume that all will be well with you. That the doctor even thinks that it's possible is wolf-god's blessing on your union with Jason."

"It's a good word," Vale agreed. "'Possible.' Full of the future. I wish Jason could embrace it."

"He will. Eventually. But know that he's stubborn."

"Oh, I know."

"He's not going to give up on changing your mind. Not for a few days yet. Maybe another week." Miner narrowed his eyes thoughtfully, obviously casting back. "Once Yule tried for nearly a full month before giving in. Though, of course, nothing could budge me back then. That was many years before you came into our lives. Jason probably doesn't remember it." He sighed. "That was right before I started taking the abortifacients regularly. I ended up in the hospital. The baby, of course, didn't live."

"I'm sorry for all you've been through."

Miner exchanged his toothpick for a new one. "I have Jason. He was worth everything."

Vale touched Miner's knee. "I agree."

Miner laughed. "I know." Then he sobered again. "I also know we should focus on the positive and not allow negative thoughts to cloud our minds. It's the traditional omega way of dealing with pregnancy. But just for now, let's be frank with each other: how good are the odds?"

"I don't know. But Urho would never have given me hope if he didn't feel they were very good odds. He'd have told me I couldn't sustain the pregnancy and insisted I…" Vale trailed off.

"And would you have gone along with his suggestion?"

Trying to think of what he would have done, Vale finally nodded. "I would have accepted his assessment."

"And terminated."

Superstitious anxiety settled on Vale, and he shrugged, refusing to entertain the thought. "It doesn't matter now. I don't have to. I get to try."

Miner nodded, understanding in his glimmering eyes. He took hold of Vale's hand and squeezed. "This baby is wonderful news, Vale. *Wonderful.*"

"IT'S AWFUL," JASON said, miserably, staring up at the clouds drifting in front of the pale sun and across the flat, blue sky. "*Awful.*"

The slanted roof beneath his old bedroom window had always been his safe place, and so he hadn't been surprised when someone had followed him out onto the slates. The fact that it was his father instead of Vale had been a bit unexpected, though.

Father tilted his head back and gazed up at the clouds, too. "I know."

"Vale won't budge. I know he won't. He's made up his mind, and I already know what happens when he does that."

Father shrugged. "He'd made up his mind not to contract with you, but you convinced him anyway."

Jason sighed. "Did I? Or did he go into heat and by the time it was over, he just didn't have it in him to reject me anymore?"

Father chuckled. "I suppose we'll never know. Omegas are hard to understand. That heat was well-timed for what you wanted. It made him realize that he couldn't stand living without you."

Jason nodded, deciding not to bring up how vigorously his

father had fought against Jason's contract with Vale, wanting him to take a younger, more fertile surrogate, and live without his *Érosgápe* forever in favor of an heir.

"It was significantly less well-timed for what he claimed to want at the time. But omegas want their alphas. *Érosgápe* are notoriously hard to keep apart." Father sobered. "But one thing's for sure… This last heat was not well-timed at all. Obviously."

"I was so scared," Jason whispered. There weren't many people in this world he was willing to admit that to. He was an alpha and had his pride. Everyone might *know* he was scared, but he hated saying it, which was idiotic because even stoic Urho had declared himself frightened.

But here with his father, knowing that he understood this particular type of terror, he could let it out. "I'm really fucking scared, Father."

Yule put his arm around Jason's shoulders and sat there in silence, letting him soak in his support.

"What do I do?"

"You have to love him. You must support him. He's an omega, and he'll need your care, your tenderness, and affection. He'll need your confidence in him, too. You must come to see this as wonderful."

"Wonderful? It's a mistake."

"Vale is making the right choice, son. He—"

"How can you say that!" Jason knocked his father's arm off his shoulder. "He's putting his life at risk because he thinks I want this baby."

"And don't you?"

"Not more than I want Vale."

Yule clucked. "Vale is smart, Jason. Very smart. He isn't going to make this choice lightly. He knows Dr. Chase well. If he heard him say things that warrant hope, then I believe he knows he has a very good chance. No omega is completely safe—"

Jason groaned.

"But if Dr. Chase gave Vale the go-ahead, then his chances must be as good as any."

"Urho never said that."

"Of course not. He's a doctor. He can't have you coming back around later if…if the worst happens."

Jason buried his face in his hand. His heart pounded. "I love him more than life. Need him more than water. More than air."

"I know. Believe me, I know."

"I'd be happily childless so long as I could have him with me for the rest of my days."

"He's older than you son."

Jason shook his head, already knowing where that was going. "I don't want to hear about that."

"You can't deny it forever."

Jason shrugged. *Just watch me.*

Father went on, "If this works out, not only will Vale have the joy of giving you a son, but when it *is* his time, he'll know he's left a piece of himself behind for you to live for."

"No."

"Hear me out—"

"No!"

Jason scrambled to his hands and knees and crawled back into his old room. It still held the bed and the desk where he'd done his schoolwork, but otherwise, the room was stripped bare of his old things. He'd taken it all to Vale's when they contracted.

"Do you remember when I bought you the microscope?" Yule asked, grunting as he followed Jason through the window and into the room. He steadied himself and regained his balance before taking Jason's arm and steering him to the bed.

Jason sat down reluctantly. "Yes."

"I told you that our world was to the universe like the cell to the world. I told you that our lives were like that, too. A drop in the continuum of life."

Jason shook his head. He had no idea where his father was going with this, but he didn't want to hear it. Why didn't anyone understand what he was feeling? Why did everyone want him to accept this choice?

"In the end, none of us matter."

"Vale matters."

"To you."

Jason glared at his father. "To the world. He's a poet. A teacher. A friend. My *Érosgápe*."

"Yes. At this moment in time, Vale matters to many people, but in fifteen years? Twenty?"

Jason worked his mouth open and scraped out, "What are you trying to say to me? That it doesn't matter if he lives or dies? This is morbid. I don't like it."

"I'm saying it's going to be all right."

Jason choked out a laugh. "Everything you just said was the least 'all right' thing I've ever heard."

Father smiled and stroked his hand through Jason's hair. "Because you're young yet. Wait until you're old. Then you'll see what I mean. Vale probably knows."

"Vale isn't old."

Father leaned in to kiss Jason's forehead. "Come on, son. Let's return to our omegas. They'll have talked in our absence. Who knows what plans they made to bring you around?"

Jason followed his father downstairs, feeling like an infant. He didn't get how everyone was so calm and so very stupid about this. Especially Vale. And Urho. And Pater. And Father.

He set his jaw stubbornly and trailed his father into the conservatory again, to find Vale and Miner on the sofa together, quietly discussing baby names.

Jason again thought he might hate Vale just a little beneath all of this smothering love. Then Vale looked up at him, his green eyes so soft with worry and a kind of hope. He clearly wanted Father to have gotten through to him in some way, and Jason's entire body flooded with adoration. He couldn't hate Vale no matter how much this choice terrified him.

Jason took Vale's chin, beard soft on his fingers, and lifted his face to plant a soft kiss on his lips. "Let's get you home. It's been a long day."

"Yes," Vale agreed readily.

They said their goodbyes, and as they left, Jason wrapped his arm around Vale's waist protectively. Vale leaned into his side, and Jason kissed the top of his head. His omega.

His.

His.

THE VISIT TO Urho's clinic and then Jason's parents' house had exhausted Vale. He collapsed onto their bed still fully clothed, and his eyes fell shut almost immediately. Jason had disappeared to the kitchen insisting that Vale must be hungry, though he was more nauseous than anything else. The pamphlets Urho had given him said this was normal as his body adapted to the baby with hormone surges.

Eventually, he heard Jason's feet on the stairs, and he woke from his light doze. His stomach rolled over, anxiety adding to his sick feeling. He hoped that Jason hadn't brought anything especially pungent for him to eat. He might not be able to keep it down.

"Hungry?" Jason asked as he sat down on the bed, stroking Vale's hair out of his face and smoothing his fingers down his dark beard. He didn't have anything with him at all. "I made a lasagna. Want to come downstairs?"

"Not really." Vale smiled pitifully. Just the thought of all that cheesiness made him feel like hurling.

"You have to eat and stay strong," Jason murmured, kissing Vale's temple.

"Some crackers and soup?" Vale asked, feeling bad that Jason had spent time making something that he was certain wouldn't sit well with him.

Jason nodded and started to rise, but Vale pulled him back down.

"Come here," he said. "Lie down with me?"

Jason complied, turning on his side to face Vale, who turned to face him, too. Their foreheads touched, and Vale closed his eyes, breathing in and out with the same rhythm as Jason.

"You can fight this for a few more days," Vale said quietly. "I'll give you until the end of the week. But then you must be stronger. You're the alpha, Jason. I'll need you to embrace that role."

Jason didn't move. They kept breathing together.

Vale spoke again, "Omegas need an alpha for their pregnancy. They need to feel cared for, supported, and there's the sexual component."

Jason swallowed audibly but remained silent.

"For me, it won't be just about the natural increase in the sex drive of a pregnant omega, or your need as an alpha to protect, pleasure, and prepare me for birth by regular intercourse. It'll be about keeping the scars stretched and flexible. It will be life or death."

Jason whimpered softly.

"So, there will still need to be a lot of fisting—a lot of fucking. And I'll need you to be excited, optimistic, and enthusiastic. I can't have negative thoughts in my head and get through this safely. You have to believe in me."

Jason clutched Vale closer, his fingers hurting where he gripped Vale's hips.

"So, one week. That's all I'll give you. Then you will turn this around. I'll need you so much by then."

Jason huffed a shallow, shaky breath. Then kissed Vale's forehead, rose, and left the room, presumably to prepare the crackers and soup. Vale stretched out on the bed and stared out the window, unsurprised when Zephyr hopped onto the mattress and curled up next to Vale's still-flat belly, purring her happy little heart out.

CHAPTER SEVEN

VALE SAT PERCHED on the leather wingback chair, his stomach twisting anxiously as Xan followed Jason into the room. The sun shone through the wide back windows of his dusty, brick-floored study, but it was the fire in the hearth that illuminated their gathered friends' tense faces.

"Glad you could join us," Vale said to Xan with a small, dry-lipped smile.

Xan's blue eyes were wide with worry, and his gaze darted between Vale and Jason, and then over to their other assembled guests—Rosen, Yosef, and Urho. Oh, even distracted as he was, Vale didn't miss that flicker of interest in Xan's eyes as he took Urho in.

"Sorry if I kept everyone waiting," Xan said shakily. "But I came as soon as I got Jason's call."

"And how's Caleb?" Vale asked, not entirely surprised Xan's omega hadn't come along but wishing that he had all the same. He could use another omega's hand to hold right about now.

"Caleb's good," Xan said, his attention too obviously split between worry for Jason and his nervous interest in Urho. "Well, he wasn't feeling well this morning, so I had to run to the drug store for a tonic for him, which made me late to work, and so it was harder to escape this afternoon."

"It's all right," Vale said. "Tell Caleb we hope he gets well soon. Rosen just arrived, too."

Jason stood behind Vale, his hands gripping the back of the

wingback chair. His presence was so tense Vale could sense his anxiety without turning to look up at him.

Vale's best friends, Rosen and Yosef, sat closely together on the leather sofa, hands intertwined, and fairly miserable expressions on their faces. Yosef's impeccably sculpted white hair and beard gave away that he was quite a few years older than Rosen, but they were still an unfailingly attractive couple. Vale had been through so much with them, weathered the worst storms of his life in their care, and hoped they would be able to support him through one more.

Xan ran a sweaty palm over his limp hair. "So, what's going on?" Xan asked, obviously unable to keep quiet a moment longer. "What the hell's happening?"

Urho stepped forward, hands clasped in front of him solemnly like one of the Holy Church of Wolf's ministers. "I've been asked to impart the news. It's both an honor and a burden, but one Jason and Vale have asked me to bear—"

"Just tell us," Xan interrupted. Vale understood, he was impatient to get the news out, too.

Urho's chin came up, and he gazed at Xan for a long, calm moment before nodding. "All right. As it turns out, Vale, against all odds and despite Jason's best efforts, is pregnant."

The silence in the room echoed off the windows, and Jason came around the side of the chair to squeeze Vale's shoulder in support.

"Excuse me?" Xan said, blinking. "Did you say Vale is pregnant?"

"I did." Urho's strong mouth drew into a straight line, and he regarded them all seriously. "This is obviously a problem, one that is both private and communal in that we all love and admire Jason and Vale, and will—"

"What in wolf's own hell, Jason?" Xan snapped, interrupting

Urho again. "You know he can't have children. Why would you knock him up?"

Jason's head and shoulders curved, but he didn't let go of Vale's shoulder as he said, "It was an accident."

"An accident?" Xan scoffed.

Irritation flashed in Vale. No one could fault Jason for what happened. Not while he was around. Vale raised his palm. "What's done is done. Now all that's left is to deal with what's happened."

"You'll have an abortion, obviously," Xan said, nodding firmly and casting an approving glance toward Urho.

He'd been there when Urho had performed the surgery on Jason's pater that had saved the man's life four years earlier. He also knew that Urho was the doctor responsible for performing an abortion on Vale when he was a young, unmatched omega.

"No," Vale whispered. "That's not going to happen this time."

"Excuse me?" Yosef asked, his white eyebrows shooting to his hairline. "What are you saying, Vale?"

Rosen straightened where he sat, gripping Yosef's hand until his knuckles went white. Xan looked a little woozy where he stood.

"Please," Jason whispered. "Please reconsider."

Vale shook his head. "Urho's examined me, and he thinks—"

"I don't care what he thinks!" Jason exclaimed, coming around to kneel at Vale's feet. "I only want you. I don't need this from you. I don't even want a ch—"

Vale put a hand over his mouth. "Shush, before you say something you'll regret."

Jason's blue eyes went wet, and he ducked his head, resting his forehead on Vale's knee. He shuddered as Vale ran his fingers through his blond hair soothingly. It was hard to be strong like this. He needed Jason to step up, to get past this, to support him. In time, he knew he would…until then, he'd offer what comfort he could.

"I don't understand," Yosef said again. "Vale can't survive a pregnancy. We all know that."

"Historically, that was true," Urho said. "Before Jason."

"So, you're saying things have changed?" Rosen murmured, lifting his chin. It was dark with late afternoon stubble and flecked with some blue paint he hadn't entirely scrubbed free. In all likelihood, he'd been pulled away from his oil painting by Jason's phone summons.

Urho said, "For reasons that are best kept private, it does seem that there is a new elasticity to Vale's scar tissue and passage that wasn't there before. I have several theories as to why that is, but the fact remains that it is, unexpectedly, true."

"I can't carry to full term, most likely," Vale said as calmly as possible, wanting to minimize the sound of danger for Jason's sake. But Jason scooted closer, burying his face further in Vale's lap, his body shaking as Vale went on. "So, Urho will induce labor early, and we'll hope the child survives."

"That's sick," Xan spat, widening his stance and glaring. "You can't do that. Not to Jason." He shot a pointed glance at Jason, where he curled by his Vale's feet. "Look at him. Think of what losing you would do to him."

Vale's heart softened. "I think of almost nothing else."

"Could have fooled me."

Vale barely restrained a flare of temper, but he managed to hold it back. "It hasn't been an easy decision, but I trust Urho. He wouldn't put the odds on me surviving if he didn't believe it with his whole heart."

Jason lifted his head then, his face blotchy with tears and his mouth wobbly. "He doesn't put odds on you surviving, he puts odds on you *probably* not dying, and that's not at all the same thing."

"Darling, you can't ask me to give this up. Unplanned as it was, as terrified as we both are, this is our only hope. This one, beautiful mistake that we'd never, ever make again."

"Don't get poetic on me," Jason whispered fiercely. "You're willing to risk destroying yourself—us, *me*—for something that, according to Urho, is just a bundle of cells with a tiny little heartbeat."

"But he's ours," Vale said urgently. "Our bodies knitted together to make a new life. How can we choose to end it?"

"You sound like Pater."

"No, your pater admitted he had no hope of living through the birth. I plan to follow all of Urho's prescriptions to the letter. I intend to live to see our child born, to hold him and raise him into a fine young man. To see you reflected in him, and myself, too. I won't be giving up so easily."

"So why are we here?" Yosef asked gently, his hands still twined with Rosen's and his expression grave.

"Because we'll need your support," Vale said. "Jason, especially."

"No, you, especially," Jason whispered. "You must be cared for every moment of every day."

"Ridiculous. I'm not an invalid." Vale shrugged. "Later, as the months pass, yes, I will need to be careful, but right now I'm as fit as a fiddle. I can continue my work—"

"No!" Jason snarled, lifting his head and glaring up at him. "I won't have those idiot alphas at Mont Nessadare scenting you and knowing you're pregnant—that you're fragile." He shook his head hard. "You'll take another leave of absence."

Vale soothed Jason again, bringing his head back into his lap and gently tracing his ear. "We'll need your help," Vale said, meeting everyone's eye one by one. "I can't say when or exactly how, but you're the friends we know we can count on for anything."

"We're always here for you," Rosen agreed.

"For you and Jason both," Yosef said grimly.

"You can count on me," Xan added, lifting his chin. "For anything at all. If I can provide comfort or support, I'm happy to do it. And Caleb will want to help, too."

"Thank you," Vale said as he rubbed Jason's shoulders. "We're struggling with this, but we'll be all right."

Jason rose then, wiping a hand over his face, rubbing away tears. "We wanted you to find out from us directly, face-to-face."

"And your parents?" Yosef asked.

"Already know," Jason replied. The way he mashed his full lips together made it clear he didn't intend to say more on that subject right now.

Rosen and Yosef were the first to depart. Yosef hugged Jason and whispered to Vale about pulling legal paperwork together regarding his health care if Jason wasn't able to make decisions. Vale nodded and then accepted a hug from Rosen, too.

Urho offered to walk Rosen and Yosef out to catch their taxi.

Xan approached them with a sympathetic smile before it slid away from him, revealing his discombobulated confusion.

Vale leaned forward to grip Xan's hand. "Don't look like that. Jason will need your strength."

Xan huffed. "Not half as much as he needs you, period. But I'll do what I can."

Vale smiled and turned to Jason. "Why don't you walk Xan out? If it's all the same to you, I'll stay here and get comfy by the fire."

"Are you cold?" Jason asked, his voice strained with emotion and thwarted need to caretake. Vale wasn't cold, but he said nothing and let Jason grab a throw blanket from the leather sofa. It was important Jason be allowed to care for him now to soothe their mutual fears, and so he smiled lovingly as Jason carefully draped the blanket over Vale, taking his time to wrap him up and tuck the blanket in carefully.

Zephyr slipped into the room. Her silvery fur was clean and fluffy, and she meowed as she trotted toward them and leapt onto Vale's lap. Freeing his hand from the blanket's wrap, Vale slipped his fingers into her fur.

"I'll be right back," Jason whispered, and then turned to Xan, his expression wrecked and yearning. "Thanks for coming. I'll walk you out."

Vale watched them go, hoping that Xan would be able to give Jason what he needed now: a friend to lean on, a strong heart to confide in. At least he knew Xan loved Jason. If there were a friend among the bunch who would be there for Jason if the worst occurred, it would be Xan.

Yes, their friends had taken the news of Vale's pregnancy better than Vale had thought they would. There'd been palpable fear and concern, but in the end, they'd all leant their support. And Vale was grateful to Xan who still loved Jason, had far too much of a crush on Urho and basically envied Vale his entire life.

Even this. Vale put his hand over his stomach, pondering the child inside. Yes, Xan would have wanted even this baby, at even the potentially-high cost Vale faced for it.

And that, surprisingly, gave Vale a sense of peace. It would be all right. He was sure of it.

Jason was not going to budge about Vale continuing his work as a teacher on a campus full of alphas. Not while he was pregnant, anyway. Vale knew that. If Jason would be more positive in general about this entire pregnancy, then it was a concession Vale would happily make. Staying home to grow their child, eating Jason's food, enduring his pampering. Napping. Reading. Writing. He'd happily do all of that if Jason supported him.

He'd call the headmaster of Mont Nessadare tomorrow and let

him know the situation. They'd find someone to cover his classes easily enough. There had long been a list of alphas waiting for his job to come open. This was, perhaps, their chance because Vale couldn't say if he would want to go back to teaching after the baby came. He never thought he'd be able to have a child, and the miracle of it seemed like something he didn't want to miss even a single second of. And yet, he'd never considered himself the kind of man to walk away from an interesting career.

When Jason returned, he apologized for the delay by saying Urho had waylaid him on the sidewalk. He didn't tell Vale what they'd talked about, but it seemed clear that whatever Urho had said finally made Jason understand that, despite his fears, this was going to happen, and he'd better start acting as an alpha should.

Because with only a bit of the strain leaking through his strong demeanor, Jason did just that.

CHAPTER EIGHT

AFTER THAT DAY, Jason was an exemplary alpha. There were no more tears or pleading speeches. Instead, he helped Vale impart the news of his sabbatical to his boss, and then went with him to campus to clear out his office. Jason insisted on carrying every box, and indulging Vale's every whim, including stopping by his favorite grilled cheese food stall on their way back home.

Vale could almost pretend that they had planned this pregnancy. He could almost convince himself that Jason was happy. But there were cracks in which the fear slipped through, despite his baby alpha's best efforts.

And that, Vale believed, was only human.

One afternoon, Jason started a casserole in the oven, played with Zephyr, and then went out to his garden to putter around, cleaning up fallen autumn leaves and babying the winter-ready flowers he'd already planted. He sang softly under his breath—a ballad from the latest musical they'd attended at the theater.

Vale listened to him through the partly open window that let in a cool breeze. Urho had closed it during his last visit, claiming the dampness might harm him, but Vale knew that was an old omega's tale. He felt better with the air circulating, the scent of autumn in the air, dispelling a bit of the heat from the banked fire. He lounged on the sofa, watching Jason move through the garden and admiring his alpha's fine form.

"Come here," Jason said from outside the window. He pushed the sash up all the way and ducked down to stick his head in the room. "Come on. Now."

Vale chewed on the inside of his lower lip to keep from smiling. Once, forever ago now, Jason had come to him at that very window and dared to break courting protocols for just a few minutes of Vale's time and his words. Oh, Jason had been so young then. And Vale had been the one who'd been afraid.

He rose from the sofa and went to the window, his heart fluttering. "Yes?"

"Kneel," Jason said in a very no-nonsense way. All command but no cruelty to it.

Vale's nipples rose beneath his loose t-shirt, and his cock began to stiffen. This, too, brought back some fond memories from their early days. Filthy and fond as fuck. "Now what?" he asked, breathlessly.

"Open your mouth."

Vale complied, his heart trip-hammering, and blood rushing to his prick. If this was what Jason needed to feel in control, to step into his alphaness, then Vale would give it eagerly.

Jason produced a brown fig, broken open and ripe. He placed some of the gooey center on Vale's tongue. Its sweet flavor burst in his mouth, and he let it sit there, waiting for Jason to tell him what to do next.

"Well, eat it," Jason said with a laugh. His eyes, which had looked so sad before, twinkled for the first time since their mountain trip. "Were you expecting something else on your tongue? Something bigger?"

Vale chewed and swallowed, narrowing his eyes. "Brat. You know I was."

"Open again."

Vale complied, but irritably this time. He didn't want figs. He wanted Jason's cock and his jizz and the pleasurable orgasm Jason was sure to give him in return. And he wanted the reassuring tenderness that would inevitably follow.

Jason placed more of the gooey fig center in his mouth, and Vale ate it without being told. "Good. Now lick my fingers clean," he said with a hint of gruffness to his voice, and that sparked Vale's cock back to life.

Closing his eyes, Vale knelt by the window and sucked all the sweet, seedy fig from Jason's fingers, his tongue working over the digits, and hollowing his cheeks so that the soft insides rubbed against Jason's flesh. There was the taste of flesh, fig, and autumn dirt, and he squirmed as slick burst from his hole, wetting his underwear and opening his hole for Jason's use.

"Ah, you like that," Jason murmured. "I smell you opening for me."

Vale nodded.

"You want me to fuck you, baby?"

Vale whimpered, his whole body going tight all over with need. Nipples taut, cock hard, balls rising up…yes, he wanted that. But he kept sucking on Jason's fingers, letting the way his eyes rolled back into his head, and the scent of slick leaking freely to answer for him.

Jason pulled his fingers loose, and as he'd done once before, climbed in through the window to kneel with Vale on the carpet. "Get your shirt off and pants down."

Vale obeyed quickly.

Jason dragged him close, body to body so that he could feel Jason's big cock shoved up against his stomach. The softness of Jason's work shirt against his torso and the roughness of his jeans against Vale's balls was intoxicating. "Repeat after me."

Vale swallowed, confused, but nodded.

"I'm healthy and strong."

Vale murmured the words back.

"I'm going to live a long time for my *Érosgápe*."

Vale leaned closed, took a long sniff of Jason's neck, scenting his delicious, one of a kind odor, and whispered, "I'm going to live a long time for you, baby alpha."

"Forever. With me."

"Yes. Forever."

Jason growled and slipped one hand around Vale's waist to hold him steady, before sliding his other hand between Vale's legs and pressing all four fingers into Vale's wet hole. It was tight, and a surprise to be invaded so thoroughly by most of Jason's hand, but Vale relaxed and let it happen. Jason worked his thumb in next, and then the widest part of his hand, letting Vale use gravity to take it fully inside. Then he curled his fingers together and, with a sigh of relief, he let Vale rest there on his fist.

"Feel that?"

"I don't see how I couldn't," Vale replied breathlessly. His cock ached in the space between their bodies, and he hunched his hips forward to get contact causing Jason's fist to move inside him, too. "It's all so much."

"Make yourself come on my hand."

Vale whimpered, but wrapped one arm around Jason's neck, and let his other drop to take hold of his cock. He jerked it quickly, not wanting to hold back, eager for a quick rocket to glory.

Jason carefully twisted his hand around inside, the position making it difficult, but the movement was enough to send Vale into the sky. He threw his head back, groaned, and shuddered hard as his body clenched on Jason's fist, and his cock erupted between them. Cum striped over Jason's soft flannel shirt and Vale crowed as his nipples sang in pleasure, and his asshole convulsed on Jason's wrist.

"Mmm," Jason murmured, leaning low to nuzzle Vale's neck. "Smells so good."

Vale's breath came in harsh, short pants, his body zinging with residual pleasure, and he scrambled to cling to Jason's shoulders as he moved his fist around inside again. "Oh, darling, you feel so good."

Vale's thighs began to shake as Jason withdrew his hand, a gasp leaving Vale's lungs in a whoosh as he felt the frustrating emptiness. "Jason, please." He didn't know what he was begging for. He'd just come, he was in his alpha's arms, and he felt fantastic. But he wanted more.

"Elbows and knees," Jason said, spinning him around.

Disoriented Vale complied, pushing his ass up into lordosis position.

"Wolf-god, you kill me," Jason whispered. The sound of his zipper was very promising, and Vale pressed his face to the carpet as he waited.

Jason always felt so right inside him. Thick, wide enough at the base to make Vale break out in a sweat every time, and long enough to brush against his womb even when it wasn't descended for heat.

"Hang on," Jason said with a growl. "I'm gonna work you open."

Vale gasped as the first thrust took him to a higher plane of reality. Chills broke over him in blissful rushes. His nipples positively ached with pleasure as Jason pummeled his ass, working his big dick deep, again and again. Jason focused the head of his cock toward the area inside where Vale had once been too tender and tight to find pleasure, but now Jason fit easily, and Vale shook and trembled, legs shaking, hips vibrating, and stomach muscles twitching, as Jason fucked him toward an anal orgasm.

He sometimes wondered what it was like to be an alpha, to be so restricted in pleasure. But at times like these, Vale was grateful to be an omega—his body was made so wonderfully and so eager for pleasure.

"That's right," Jason said when Vale stopped crooning and

convulsing. "You're my omega. My *Érosgápe*."

"Always," Vale agreed, and when Jason used his body weight to shove them both to the floor, the soft flannel of Jason's shirt rubbed deliciously against Vale's naked back.

Jason held Vale's hips, shoved deep inside, and came with a cry. His big cock pulsed hard, and the gushes of semen filled Vale up and slipped out along with the slick he'd produced. He could feel the throbbing head of Jason's convulsing dick pressed against the tightly closed mouth of his womb.

"Wolf-god." Jason groaned and rolled them to their sides so that Vale could more easily breathe. "I love fucking you."

"The feeling is mutual."

They breathed in silence, their bodies still twitching with pleasure for several long minutes. Jason pressed a kiss to the back of Vale's neck. "I can smell him."

"I know."

"It's different from your smell alone."

"Yes."

"It almost obscures it. Like I wouldn't recognize you…if he wasn't mine because he smells like mine—ours."

Vale nodded. He'd heard omegas talk about the alpha's reaction to the scent of their unborn child. He'd had an omega friend, widowed while pregnant, tell him that the alpha who took care of him through his pregnancy claimed he smelled entirely different once the child was born.

Jason sighed and slowly withdrew, pressing a few fingers back inside for Vale to squeeze against, and then after Vale nodded his readiness, pulled free entirely, helping Vale rise unsteadily to his feet. As they fixed their clothes back in place, Jason kept kissing Vale's cheek, the side of his mouth, and his earlobes. Vale couldn't stop smiling.

"Let's shower and then I'll make dinner."

"I never got my nap," Vale complained, looking longingly toward the sofa.

"Oh? You'd rather nap than see what I'm going to do to you in the shower?"

Vale hesitated. "There's more?"

"So much more."

Vale slipped his arm through Jason's. "Lead the way."

Halfway up the stairs, Jason said, "I love him, you know? I do. I already love him."

Vale tugged him to a halt and pulled Jason's head down to grab another kiss. "Thank you."

Jason snorted. "Like I ever had a choice when it came to you."

Vale smiled and rubbed his beard against Jason's cheek. "Nor I when it came to you. It was you pouncing on me in the library if I recall correctly."

"If you could have smelled yourself, you'd have pounced on you, too."

Vale laughed, letting Jason pull him up the stairs and into the shower. They made love again, and this time when Vale came, he couldn't help the tears of pleasure and gratitude slipping down his wet face.

CHAPTER NINE

B Y THE TIME Jason arrived home from work, he had finally shaken off a bit of the bewilderment he'd faced when Urho had accosted him on the sidewalk that morning. For most of the day, he'd thought about Urho's desperate eyes as he'd unwittingly revealed to Jason his tormented attraction to Xan. As he put dinner together, having left Vale reading a novel in the study, Jason considered what trouble Xan might have gotten himself into, and what alpha he might be seeing who would frighten Urho so much.

"That smells wonderful," Vale said as he slipped into the kitchen. He wore a robe over pajamas just as he had since Urho had confirmed the pregnancy. He was truly a decadent man and enjoyed the pampering, but Jason knew it was only a matter of time before Vale started to feel stir-crazy and demanded to go out and about. He wouldn't be surprised to come home from work one day soon to discover a note announcing Vale had gone to his beta friends, Yosef and Rosen's house to visit. At least Jason knew they were responsible, reliable men who'd make sure Vale ate well and stayed calm.

"Sheet pan sausage and veggies," he said, putting the pan in the oven, and adjusting the temperature. "Thirty minutes."

"Just enough time for you to tell me why you're frowning."

"Ah, it's complicated."

"I'm feeling great," Vale said defensively. "My nausea has settled. I'm hungry. I feel strong and healthy."

"It's not about the pregnancy, actually," Jason said slowly. "It's about Urho. And Xan."

Vale's lips twitched into a smirk. "They need someone to lock them together in a closet. Naked. Ten minutes later, they would resolve the problem between them."

"So, you know?"

"Of course. I'm not blind."

"I suppose I have been. It never occurred to me until today, but…"

"The electricity when they are near each other could light all the bulbs in our house," Vale said. "I wish they'd just give in."

"Urho isn't quite ready yet, I don't think."

"He always did have to drag everything out. There were times…" Vale trailed off and then shrugged, obviously rethinking his next sentence which told Jason it was probably a reference to the sexual relationship he'd once had with Urho. "It's simply his way to cling to protocol, propriety, and the past. Even after all these years, he hasn't forgiven himself for his *Érosgápe's* death." Vale's lips tightened. "It was tragic, but Urho couldn't have stopped it if he'd tried.

"How was the lab this morning? Did the microbes react the way you thought they would? To the, uh, fizzy stuff you were soaking them in?"

Jason smiled. Vale was always sweetly trying to get his mind around Jason's pet projects, but he didn't care about it deeply, and the details of it went over his head. If Jason had wanted to spend his hours dissecting sonnets, Vale would have been able to hold his own and even teach Jason a thing or two. But when it came to lab work, Vale was very much bored. So, it was adorable to see him try. "I didn't go in. Hopefully Dr. Obi will forgive me. You know he's a stickler for punctuality. Hopefully, he'll let me continue to work with him."

"Since you do it all for free, I'm sure he will. But what kept you?"

"Urho. He grabbed me off the sidewalk and interrogated me about my former relationship with Xan. I'd never seen him like that before. Frankly, if I hadn't known him, I'd have thought he was out of his mind. He looked like he hadn't slept in days." Jason frowned, getting out cups to pour water and some special, stomach-settling tea for Vale. "I think whatever he's feeling, it's stronger than he wants to admit."

"So, you told him about you and Xan being lovers before?"

Jason sighed. "I did. But somehow he already knew. He was furious about it. He said I was reckless, that Xan was, too, but I think he was…jealous? It was the strangest conversation I've ever had with him."

"And?" Vale prompted, knowing Jason too well to think that was the end of it.

"He said Xan was involved with another alpha and that this relationship could spell trouble."

"Knowing Xan, I'm sure it could."

"Yeah. I'm going to head over to Xan's in the morning to look in on him. Make sure he hasn't gotten himself into anything he shouldn't have." Jason sighed heavily. "I hoped that after he contracted with Caleb, he'd change."

"Darling, it's just who he is. He's never going to want an omega the way you do. I only hope it isn't too onerous for Caleb. But I've heard rumors about him. Omegas talk."

"What kind of rumors?"

"Just that he might be the perfect fit for Xan in a lot of ways."

Jason eyed Vale, but he knew he wasn't going to get more out of him that night. Instead, he turned his thoughts back to Xan. "I know what you're saying about Xan's nature, and I agree. But he's so impulsive."

"He has a bit of a death wish," Vale agreed.

"Does he?" Jason asked, his heart skipping a beat. "Would he put himself in that kind of serious danger?"

"I don't know, darling, but Xan struggles with himself more than any other alpha I've ever met."

"I need to check on him tomorrow."

"Of course, you do. You'll take care of him. You always have."

"I took care of him too well, maybe. That's what Urho thinks," Jason said softly. His memories of the hours he and Xan spent naked and enjoying their bodies together flipped through his mind. It had meant so much less to him, and so much more to Xan. He still felt guilty to have broken his best friend's heart.

"Urho is often a fool. I thought you knew that by now," Vale said, rising from the table and coming to put his arms around Jason. "A very stubborn, blind fool."

Jason let Vale kiss his neck, and then he pulled away to set the table. "No distractions. You're going to eat tonight, and you're going to eat well."

Vale crossed his finger over his chest, "Cross my heart or poke a needle in wolf-god's eye."

Jason put aside his worry for his friend and concentrated on taking care of his beautiful, pregnant *Érosgápe*. He could see just the smallest start of a bulge in Vale's abdomen. He wasn't even sure it had been there yesterday. He wanted to kneel down and kiss it.

He wanted to keep Vale and the baby safe. And Xan, too.

But for now, all he could do was make sure Vale ate his dinner. And so, he would.

VALE FINGERED HIMSELF open as he watched Jason sleep.

The pregnancy hormones had started to drive him a bit batty lately. The mere scent of Jason when he walked in the door made slick burst from his glands, and his cock grow fat. It was almost as intense as it had been when they'd first found each other, but a great deal easier than heat.

Still, the constant itch of low-grade arousal was distracting, and being woken from sleep with a hard-on and a wet hole was frustrating as wolf's own hell, especially when Jason was sound asleep and oblivious to Vale's need.

With one leg hitched on Jason's hip, he studied Jason's sleeping face—golden lashes pressed against his high cheekbones, lips still puffy from the long blow job he'd administered to Vale at bedtime, and that flush to his cheeks that made him look almost as young as the day they'd met. Vale let out a soft moan, shoving as deep as he could inside himself, pressing against his sensitive slick glands, and twitching his hips back and forth against the pads of his fingers. It wasn't as deep or as good as when Jason did it for him, but it was pleasurable all the same. He slipped his other hand beneath his loose pajama shirt and tweaked his slightly swollen nipples. They were more sensitive than ever as the hormones raged in him, and he could easily come just from Jason's mouth on them now. Omegas were truly lucky that way.

The tension in his legs gave way to twitching, and he held back a groan. Jason's soft breathing picked up slightly as though he might be dreaming of something strenuous, and then his eyes popped open, blue and piercing even in moonlight.

It took only a moment for him to understand what was happening, and without a word, he turned Vale onto his back, moved between his legs and pressed his thighs back. Shoving his pajama pants down, Jason thrust inside and Vale gasped as that hard, perfectly formed cock slid in, milking his slick glands and causing his hips to start twitching convulsively.

Jason kissed his cheek and pushed his shirt up, revealing the small bulge that was showing now. He began to tweak Vale's nipples until his legs were shaking against Jason's heaving sides and pleasure exploded in him, all perfect obliteration and shivering nerve endings.

They fucked in the quiet of the night, the only noises Vale's soft cries and the slap of their bodies. Jason remained silent and calm, his body moving as hard and fast as Vale needed it and slowing again to drag out the pleasure. Time slipped by, and Vale was wet all over from sweat, slick, and his own cum. Yet Jason continued to fuck him steadily, no madness or loss of control to his rhythm.

Vale felt as though he'd lifted slightly out of his skin, pulsing with bliss that he couldn't contain, and shaking all over. His thighs and hips, his stomach and arms quivered so hard that his cries were tremulous, too. Jason was relentless, and when Vale shattered for what had to be the tenth time, and as the dawn cracked the sky open outside their bedroom window, Jason finally withdrew, took a few calming breaths, and then pushed back in with a frenzy.

He shot deep into Vale, clutching his hips, jolting with strong pulses, and shouting at the ceiling. When it passed, he fell to the side, one hand going to Vale's hole and pushing fingers inside like always, and another climbing into Vale's hair. He tugged Vale into a kiss that lasted a long time, saliva and tongues and whispers helping them down from the heights.

"Satisfied yet?" Jason said, his voice like sandpaper. "Think you can sleep now?"

Vale whimpered an answer and closed his eyes, and Jason laughed.

"Think we'll survive this pregnancy with how horny we are now?" Jason asked. "I can't keep my hands off you."

"Mmm," Vale agreed. "Neither can I."

"Given that I woke to find you with your fingers up your sweet asshole, and playing with your nipples, I believe that."

"I meant off you," Vale said. "But I guess I'm guilty as charged."

"Nothing to be guilty of. That was the sexiest thing I've ever woken to see. In fact, just thinking about it is making me a little hard again."

Vale huffed. "Oh, no, darling. Not more. I'm wrung out."

Jason smirked and leaned over, licking Vale's nipples. "Are you sure? Not one more round? We haven't fucked until dawn since the first year." His tongue tickled Vale's nipple again, and his asshole quivered eagerly.

"Oh, wolf-god, you're a brat."

Jason committed himself to Vale's nipples and before long Vale was begging for Jason to slide his cock back inside. There was no other pleasure as profound as Jason's body inside his own. No other joy. Except perhaps knowing that he grew inside his womb the knitted together proof of their love.

CHAPTER TEN

Two weeks later

VALE DIDN'T KNOW how to tell Jason that he was fairly certain he was going to murder Jason's parents before this pregnancy ended. He adored Miner and Yule for the most part, although they frequently forgot he wasn't that much younger than them and treated him as if he were Jason's age. But since his pregnancy, they'd become nearly unbearable, inviting themselves over nearly every day to "help out." Which really meant they came to interrogate Vale about his health, his diet, and the state of the nursery. Which Miner was especially interested in helping with, but was something they hadn't even begun to plan yet. It got so intense sometimes, with Miner touching his stomach and taking his pulse, that Vale was certain that if he'd consent to Miner doing a full-on examination of his anal passage and womb, the man would do it.

It was indeed frustrating because, until the pregnancy, he'd considered Miner one of his closest omega friends. Now he'd started to dread his visits and had almost insisted that Jason refuse them entrance when they'd showed up for dinner tonight bearing take-out and a couple of bottles of wine. Which Vale couldn't drink, but it was nice to see Jason relaxed and loose with it. And Yule, too, for that matter.

So, now, watching his father-in-law grow more and more tipsy, he was tentatively glad they'd accepted. This was a side of Yule he'd never seen before.

"How is Xan doing in Virona?" Miner asked. He hadn't been

drinking either. Vale didn't know if it was in solidarity, or if he wasn't a fan of being tipsy. He did say to Vale that earlier on in the pregnancy, Vale would find that drunk people are incredibly annoying to sober people. Saying that when he'd been pregnant and hadn't been able to indulge in liquor or wine, the more he was around people who did, the less he admired the results of alcohol.

For his part, Vale was finding it more amusing than annoying, but truly it could probably go either way depending on the person.

"Xan's doing well," Jason said. "He says Caleb is happy enough up there, too."

"That's always important," Miner said. "A happy omega means a happy home." He smiled at Vale. "Right, dear?"

Vale lifted his water glass in a toast. "Cheers to that."

When everyone had clinked and taken a drink, the conversation went on. "But why did they move?" Miner asked. "He never struck me as the type to want to leave the city. Neither did Caleb. They were both into the arts and throwing parties. What prompted it?"

Yule, flushed with wine and apparently feeling gossipy, said, "My impression, dear, is that Doxan sent him away due to some scandal or another. Do you know what it is, Vale? Jason won't tell us, of course." He took another large swallow of his wine and then added ruefully, "He's far too protective of Xan."

"Just the right amount of protective, actually," Vale countered with a raised brow.

Miner shot Yule a dark glance and then added, "I'd hope Jason was discreet about Xan, for many reasons."

Yule rolled his eyes. "Pfft. All that from when they were younger? Youthful indiscretions. That's all it was with Jason, I know. But that Xan? He was always going to be unmanned."

"Father," Jason warned quietly. "There are all sorts of reasons why this isn't something we should talk about."

"Your omega knows, doesn't he? He must." Yule lifted his wine glass and used it to indicate Vale again before taking a large swallow. "He doesn't look surprised or worried. He's aware of what boys sometimes do together."

Vale's curiosity piqued, and he fought back a smirk as he asked, "Did you ever do that with an alpha?"

Miner rolled his eyes and crossed his arms over his chest, rolling the post-dinner toothpick in his mouth. "Yule, don't answer that."

"Of course!" Yule crowed, and Jason blushed. Miner sighed and shook his head in annoyance. "I was a member of an exclusive club. We'd wrestle, get our blood up, and when the alpha expression hit…" Yule grinned, clearly delighted with the memories. "Let's just say some old-fashioned dominance was exercised on the losers most nights." His chest puffed up. "*I* never lost."

"Father," Jason murmured, his cheeks pinking prettily. Vale almost wanted to laugh at him. Alphas never expect other alphas will behave as badly as they do. Only omegas understood the truth of it. "Are you saying…that's not legal."

"We were boys," Yule said, harrumphing and flipping his hand around. "Omegas do it all the time."

"We don't *wrestle*," Miner murmured, twirling his toothpick. "If we indulge, we're much more civilized about it. Jason was civilized, weren't you, darling?"

Jason looked like his head was about to explode, and Vale covered his mouth with his napkin, holding in a giggle. Then he turned to Miner. "So, you had a Mont Juror lover?"

Vale had never indulged in physical pleasure with another omega back in the day, needing an alpha's strong scent to become truly aroused. Though of course, he'd had sex with betas sometimes after he'd graduated. Still, he was curious about his father-in-law's proclivities before contracting.

Miner shook his head. "No, of course not. Yule likes to think I did. But I didn't. I was just friends with Zander."

"He was a gorgeous man," Yule said, slurring slightly. "Stunning."

"He was my friend," Miner repeated with a sharp glare at his alpha. "But there were boys at Mont Juror who did become lovers. There was one pair who were so devoted to each other that it was quite hard on them when their parents made them contract with alphas. I hear they still vacation together, though."

"Who knows what happens behind those closed doors," Yule said with a waggle of his brows. "Decadent vacationing indeed. That's possible when you're not *Érosgápe*."

"This is embarrassing," Jason said. "Please stop."

"It's interesting," Vale said.

It was more than interesting. It was the best time he'd had with Yule and Miner in a week or more. No coddling questions like, "What have you eaten?" or "Do you need help during the day?" or "Can I sit with you tomorrow and bring you fresh fruit?" He was going to go mad if they kept doting on him so much. This filthy discovery of his in-laws' youthful debaucheries was a welcome reprieve from all of that.

At least for him. Jason looked like he wanted to die.

"There was this one alpha," Yule said. "Iri Pomeroy. A real brute of a guy. Lost the wrestling matches *all the time*, though. I swear he did it on purpose. Squealed when we fucked him, but always came in his shorts like he—"

"All right. We're leaving," Miner said, throwing his napkin down.

"Oh, no! But this was just getting good," Vale exclaimed. Jason rose as well, obviously eager to end the torture.

"I don't think any of us need to hear this," Miner muttered.

"I do!" Vale said.

Yule laughed. "See, Miner? He wants to know."

"I don't!" Jason exclaimed. "I'm going to need to drink the rest of our liquor cabinet just to get these images out of my head."

"Such a prude," Yule said to Vale with a sad shake of his head. "I hope he's not like this as your alpha."

"He's plenty filthy," Vale said with a wink.

"And now I really do want to go. Now." Miner said with a shudder. "Both of you are being too…too…" He flung his hands out as if trying to throw away their entire conversation and everything that Vale and Yule were being.

"Yeah," Jason agreed, motioning toward the door. "Thanks for bringing the takeout, but it's time to go home."

Yule sighed, kissed Vale's cheek as he passed him, and whispered, "Call me tomorrow, and I'll tell you the rest. Some very powerful men liked to bottom. I could rule this city if I wanted to name names."

"Good thing you're content to make cars," Miner said, taking Yule by the arm and tugging him away.

"I have nothing to hide," Yule said. "I never lost."

Miner just shook his head, and with Jason's help, they steered Yule toward the door. "Don't worry, I'll drive," Miner said, patting Jason's shoulder with an apologetic look. Then he turned to Vale and rolled his eyes. "As for you…I don't know why I expected you not to encourage him."

Vale smiled and rubbed his hand over his belly, which had grown quite a bit over the last few days. "I'm a bored, homebound, pregnant omega. Of course, I'm going to encourage him."

Miner bussed Vale's cheeks. "I'll be over tomorrow with fruit for you and the baby."

"You don't—"

And then he was gone, pulling Yule along with him and shaking his head as Yule continued to crow all the way to the car about the fun he'd had wrestling alphas into submission.

"I need a drink," Jason said, passing the dining room with a wave of his hands. "I'll get the plates later."

"Did you ever wrestle for the chance to—" Vale began as he sat down in the wingback chair while Jason poured a tumbler of whiskey for himself.

"No!" Jason sighed. "I never saw sex like that. The one time I felt that way, felt the alpha expression, it bothered me. I didn't want to feel that again."

"It happened with Xan?"

"At the end. The last time." He shook his head, a sad expression falling on his face. "It'd never been like that with us, and I wasn't happy about what I'd done. Or how it felt to do it. I don't understand alphas who like it."

Vale smiled as Jason took his whiskey and started to lay a fire. The room was chilly as the autumn fell deeper. Soon there would be Autumn Night Feasts to plan. Normally, he hosted one for his friends before the feast dates, then they went to Jason's parents' on the actual dates, but this year he wasn't sure.

"I love that you see sex as something sacred, even when it was with your friend."

Jason glanced over his shoulder from where he was arranging the logs. "I had plenty of sex with betas, too, you know. I admit I used them more than I ever used Xan. I'm not an angel, Vale."

"No, I suppose you're not."

"Though I didn't enjoy it much with betas. It was clear my cock hurt them." Jason shrugged. "It's better with you."

"Of course, it is. We're *Érosgápe*. Nothing compares."

"Even if we hadn't been, I'd enjoy it more with you."

"Oh, sweet baby alpha, you are too good. Come here."

"I'm not done with the fire," Jason protested.

"But my dick needs to be sucked and my asshole rimmed, and I want to come."

Jason groaned and sucked down a sip of his whiskey. "You

tempting little slut," he murmured.

Vale unbuttoned his pants and slipped them down and off. He pulled his t-shirt over his head, and by the time Jason had the fire going and turned around, Vale was naked and hard in the wing-backed chair.

"Ah damn," Jason said, standing and sipping his drink with a bulge in the front of his pants. "Look at you. All mine."

Vale ran his hands over his rounding stomach, touched his puffy nipples, and then tipped his head back with a groan. Jason knelt between his thighs and the wet heat of his mouth closing over the cut crown of Vale's dick was enough to stop the sweet need for his alpha's touch. The pressure of Jason's fingers at his asshole was the only warning he got before Jason was working him open in preparation for Vale's nightly fisting.

Just like Urho had prescribed.

CHAPTER ELEVEN

One month later

"**I**'M GOING TO murder your pater," Vale said suddenly in the middle of the night, waking Jason from a dead sleep.

"Mm, what?" Surely, he'd misheard.

"I'm going to kill him. With my bare hands."

"Baby, what are you talking about?" Jason asked, turning on the bedside lamp and rolling onto one elbow so that he could look down at Vale's beautiful, if slightly puffy, face.

"He comes here every night, Jason. Every. Single. Night."

"They're excited to be grandparents. He wants to check on you."

"And your father, too. I'm going to kill him as well. Double homicide."

Jason blinked and wiped a hand over his face in exhaustion. "Why aren't you sleeping?"

"Because that spicy quinoa your father brought over—and your pater forced me to eat—has given me the most outrageous heartburn. My esophagus and mouth are on fire."

"Let me get some milk," Jason said, crawling from the bed. "That will help."

"What will help is if your parents left me alone for one single solitary day."

Jason ignored that and went downstairs for milk, nearly tripping over Zephyr on the way down. A glance out the kitchen window showed that their neighbor's lights were still on. Frowning, Jason saw moving shadows going back and forth, like someone pacing and coughing.

After pouring the milk, Jason scooped Zephyr up into his arms, too, and carried her and the milk up to the bedroom. He kicked the door shut behind him and dumped Zephyr onto the bed by Vale, who immediately cooed and put out his hand for Zephyr to bump against. Jason put the milk down on the bedside table.

"Mr. Ragnak's beta partner has caught the flu, I think," Jason said. He sat beside Vale, putting one hand on Vale's forehead to check for fever. The other, he placed on his large, swollen abdomen, feeling for the baby's movement. Over the last few weeks, Vale's body had grown to accommodate the life rapidly expanding inside him. There had been more complaints as the days went on, mainly ligament and bone pain as his body shifted in readiness. When Jason put his fist inside now, he could feel the weight of the child bearing down on him. He worked his knuckles into the scars more vigorously each night, keeping them as limber and supple as possible as Vale's body put pressure on them.

"Oh, no," Vale murmured, stroking Zephyr's fur, calmed as usual by his cat's warm presence. "He's a good man. We should send over some fruit. And perhaps Urho."

"Urho will be here tomorrow to check on you, not them," Jason said firmly. The last thing he wanted was Urho bringing the virus into their home. "How is your stomach doing?"

"Ugh."

"Sit up. Drink this milk."

He helped Vale into position and then pressed the glass of milk into his hands. Zephyr tried to press against the glass, wanting some for herself, but Vale drained it with a few hearty gulps and then let out a big burp.

Zephyr meowed before settling herself with a sniff by Vale's side. Her tail twitched ominously, but a purr started after only a moment. Such a contrary thing. A little like Vale himself.

"Better?"

"A bit."

"We'll ask Urho about the heartburn tomorrow."

"Or you can just tell your parents not to come over."

Jason winced. He could, and maybe he should, given how much they irritated Vale with their mother-henning. But he hated to keep them away when it clearly meant so much to them to watch Vale grow and expand with their grandchild.

"I'm too hot," Vale said, kicking back the covers. It disrupted Zephyr, who jumped down and then scampered under the bed as Vale tugged off his sleep shirt. "And my nipples are tingling. They feel strange. And wet."

Jason licked his lips as a sweet scent came to his nose. Milk. Vale's milk. He groaned softly. "That's new," he murmured. "Is that supposed to happen?" He touched Vale's wet nipples with his thumbs, feeling milk seep out from beneath. "I didn't think this happened until later. After the babe's birth."

"Can happen whenever the body wants," Vale said. He squirmed a bit as Jason tweaked his nipples and watched in fascination as milk leaked from them. "Later, from what other omegas told me, it jets out with a great deal of force. Babies sometimes cough and choke on it."

Jason stared at Vale's red nubs, tweaking and playing with them as milk leaked in a small stream down his bare torso, slipping around the bulge of his stomach, and wetting the bedsheets. Vale whimpered and let him do it while rolling his hips, obviously aroused.

Jason's cock pushed against his pajama bottoms as he pressed one thumb into his own mouth, tasting the sweetness of the fluid Vale's body was making. This was to feed their child, he knew, but right now the babe was still safely tucked in Vale's womb. This sweetness could be his instead.

He took Vale's right nipple in his mouth, sucking. Sweet, creamy fluid slipped over his tongue, and he moaned. So did Vale, tangling his fingers in Jason's hair and holding him tight to his chest. "Oh, baby alpha, that's so good."

His nipples were clearly sensitive, and Jason played with the left while he tongued and gently bit the right. Vale grunted and groaned, legs twitching against the mattress, and his heart pounding loudly. The scent of slick rose up.

Jason pulled away, divested himself of his pajamas, and shoved Vale's bottoms down and off. He pushed the bedding aside completely, revealing his omega's long, lean body and shifting stomach. The baby was awake. It was awkward, sometimes, to fuck Vale while the baby was moving, but it was intriguing, too. Sometimes, when he was in so very deep, he felt the thump of the life they'd made against him, and it was always a shock, always a beautiful surprise.

"On your side," he said, helping Vale get into one of the only positions they could truly comfortably fuck in these days. Vale's expanding body made certain positions hard to hold and others impossible.

"I feel like I'm going to die if you're not inside me soon," Vale moaned, his fingers tweaking his own nipples, and his hips pushing back to allow Jason easier entry. "Make me come, darling. I want to come."

Jason pressed his body along Vale's back, hooked his chin over Vale's shoulder, and took hold of his hip to help steady him as he pushed inside. Slick heat enveloped his throbbing cock, and he moaned. "Right where I belong."

"Yes," Vale agreed. "The beginning and end."

"Alpha and omega."

The reminder of their vows warmed Jason with painful affection as he thrust in slow and deep. The tug of Vale's body around him as he pulled back out was a soul-shivering pleasure, and the hot clench as he pressed back in, milking Vale's omega glands and prostate, was sheer perfection.

"Baby, hitch your leg forward a little," he said, wanting to get inside Vale as far as possible. "I want to feel you deeper."

Vale complied, and it opened up some space for Jason to fuck him harder. The rocking of their bodies and the slap of skin on skin became a rhythm that Jason breathed to, in and out, harder and faster, until he was panting like a horse while Vale twisted on his cock and cried out. Orgasms washed over Vale, and his nipples dripped sweet milk as his asshole leaked slick.

So much wet, delicious, slick fluid. Jason reveled in it, spreading the milk around on Vale's chest and stomach, and then leaning over Vale's torso, taking his left nipple into his mouth, to suck as he fucked.

"Oh, darling," Vale gasped, his body tightening in that familiar way that said he was about to lose himself in a climax. "Oh, Jason, I'm going to…I'm going to come." And come, he did. His cock pulsed with release, his asshole gushed slick, and his nipples wetted his chest in a flood of sweetness.

Jason groaned, pulled out, and scrambled up to flip Vale onto his back. "Open your mouth."

Still squirming and coming, Vale did, and Jason aimed his pleasure right into his open mouth, pleased to see Vale greedily gulp his semen as it burst out of him and landed on Vale's teeth and tongue.

Afterward, panting and exhausted, he held Vale's body close, listening for his breathing to quiet, and sleep to overtake him again. They'd clean up tomorrow. Change the sheets. For now, he liked to sleep in their mess. The smells were so delicious.

"I think you're hornier now than ever," Vale said softly. "And they call pregnant omegas sluts. I think you're just as much to blame for all the sex we have."

"There's nothing blameful about our sex," Jason said. "It's beautiful."

"Of course, it is, darling. I just think it's amusing that I barely have time to consider initiating it before you've already pounced on me."

"You're wolf-damned delicious. That's why."

Vale smiled sleepily, and Jason kissed the edge of his mouth. "I love you."

"I love you, too." Jason put his hand over Vale's stomach. "And him."

"Yes. He's ours."

Jason still sometimes had to fight off the cold waves of fear that gripped him, especially with this flu season looking worse and worse by the day. But he had become more optimistic about Vale's chances as the weeks passed and he witnessed his omega's body do its job of making room for their son.

If anything, the scars seemed more flexible than ever. Urho posited that the hormones that made Vale's body malleable for the pregnancy also acted on the scar tissue. Jason's constant fisting and fucking were also doing their jobs of keeping him well-stretched. In the dark of their bed, fresh from orgasm, Jason could almost believe he had no reason at all to be afraid.

His child...*their* child, and his *Érosgápe* were safe and healthy. Everything was beautiful. Their life was perfect. And Vale was going to be just fine.

CHAPTER TWELVE

VALE SQUIRMED AS Urho pressed the cold stethoscope against Vale's chest. Urho hushed him and frowned.

"Everything all right?" Jason asked. His arm was around Vale's shoulder, and his eyes stayed glued to where the stethoscope pressed against Vale's skin. They were seated on the sofa in Vale's study with Urho kneeling in front of them. Vale wore a soft button-up shirt—which was now open—and drawstring paternity pants. Jason was still in his dress pants and shirt, having just returned from his work in his father's offices a few minutes before their appointment with Urho.

"Shh, I'm listening," Urho hushed again. He moved the stethoscope down to press against Vale's belly.

Jason radiated impatience.

Urho had seemed anxious lately, Vale had noticed. He didn't think it was about him or the baby. In fact, it seemed tied to Xan's move to Virona. That, along with Jason's random hints, made Vale fairly sure that Urho and Xan had entered into a relationship of the most taboo kind.

Jason huffed. "You've been listening a long time. Is there a problem?"

Urho shot him a glare, closed his eyes, and counted softly under his breath. Then he sat back on his heels. "The babe is getting along just fine, but Vale's blood pressure and heart rate are elevated. He's stressed."

"*He's* right here," Vale said testily, shifting on the sofa. His stomach had grown a lot over the prior weeks, and he could feel the child moving inside him. "I don't like being talked about like I'm not present. I'm a grown man, for wolf-god's own fucking sake."

Jason clucked gently, stroking a soothing hand over Vale's arm. "Don't get upset. It's not good for the baby."

Vale glared at Jason irritably.

Jason swallowed hard and looked down, whispering, "But, of course, we'll stop. Right away. I promise."

Vale groaned and rubbed his bulging, shifting stomach. "Is it normal for him to do that?" he asked, referring to the baby. He knew it was normal for Jason to be overprotective. All alphas were. "He head-butts my ribs and then pushes with his feet against the mouth of my womb."

"Perfectly normal."

"Well, I wish he'd stop!"

Jason rubbed Vale's shoulders and kissed his head.

"It's preparation for the life to come," Urho said. "Children rarely do what we wish they'd do. And, from what I've witnessed, their growth into adulthood is never without pain to the parent."

Vale sniffed and closed his eyes. "That's all fine and well, but I'm tired."

"I can prescribe something gentle to help you rest."

"Please do," Jason said, his fingers kneading into Vale's shoulders in a light massage. "He was up walking last night. Nothing soothed him. Not even his usual bedtime tea—the one with the herbs that make him drowsy."

"Speaking of," Vale said, as pulled away from Jason's fingers and buttoned his shirt. "I want some tea. Daytime tea. Something strong and well steeped. Jason, will you get it, please?"

Jason rose, obviously reluctant to leave Vale's side, but like any alpha, he was also prepared to do whatever his pregnant omega demanded of him. This Vale counted on because he wanted a few minutes with Urho alone.

The doorbell rang.

Vale growled, almost pulling off the final button in his annoyance. "If that's your pater or father, I will murder them both. Do you hear me? *Murder. Them. Both.*"

Jason bent to run his fingers over Vale's dark beard, whispering, "If it's them, I'll tell them to leave. I promise." Then he rushed off as the doorbell rang a second time.

Urho began to gather his things. "I'll get out of your hair, too."

"You never come over anymore except to examine me," Vale complained. He never thought he'd say it, but resting on the sofa all day, reading books and eating the food Jason had left behind for him grew a little dull. He'd been accustomed to teaching at least two units a day at the university and seeing his friends a night or two a week. Now he just saw his annoying in-laws.

"I come here every day." Urho buckled his bag and sat on the sofa next to Vale, a knowing smile on his face. "But I can stay awhile if you want."

Restlessness rose up in Vale, and he stood to pace. The baby rolled and kicked, visible even beneath Vale's loose shirt. "He moves around so much," Vale said, rubbing a hand over his stomach. "Is that normal?"

"Better than normal. It's a good sign."

"I can't stop eating. Sometimes I eat so much, I can't put any more in, but I'm still hungry."

"Another excellent sign."

"And everyone just pisses me the wolf-hell off."

"Normal enough," Urho said with a sympathetic smile. "You're uncomfortable, and the weight of the baby is putting a strain on the scar tissue now. That's enough to make anyone cranky."

Vale glanced toward the doorway out to the hallway and sighed. "Jason is adorable."

"I've heard that from you before, yes," Urho said.

"But he's making me crazy!" Vale gestured emphatically to make his point. "Eat this. Drink that. Sleep more. Let me rub your feet. Don't tax yourself. Let's read together." He snorted. "Read together. *Read* together!"

Urho raised a brow. "Did Jason not read before?"

"No! He has a photographic memory, and so he just skims books. "Vale was rather proud of his baby alpha for that trait, but still… "No, he doesn't read. Unless I read to him."

"I see."

Vale didn't like the judgment he heard in Urho's voice. Jason might not be much of a reader, but he was a very good alpha, very smart. The best of all men. "He tinkers. Out in the garden, mostly. Or with his microscope." Vale groaned. "But now he's glued to my side. Plus, he smells amazing to me. Like my alpha, yes, but I scent him even more strongly."

"This is normal."

"*This* leaves me aroused all the time." Vale threw his hands wide. "All the time, Urho!"

"I know but—"

"No but! Being aroused all the time is exhausting. Let me tell you this now. Are you listening?"

"Yes."

"I am getting *ridiculously* tired of being fisted every day."

Urho's lips quivered. "I told him to do that."

"I know." Vale crossed his arms over his chest and snarled at Urho. "Tell him to stop."

Urho sighed. "Love, it's important that you keep stretching that scar tissue. It's going to be a tough few months, but in the end, you'll have a beautiful baby, and it will be worth it."

"I know all that!" Vale exclaimed. Then it hit him. The pet name Urho had used… He turned to Urho speculatively. "Wait, though. Should you still call me that?"

"What?"

"Love? Should you call me a pet name like that?" Vale tilted his head, waiting, certain that this line of questioning would produce interesting results.

"If it bothers you, I can st—"

"No. I don't care, but does Xan mind, do you think?" He raised a brow, studying Urho's reaction.

Urho frowned. "I've called you 'love' for years—"

"Not when Jason's around."

Urho scoffed. "Because I don't have a death wish."

"So, what you have with Xan, it's not…" Vale rolled his hand, watching Urho closely.

"Nickname material?" Urho hazarded.

"No!" Vale ran a hand into his hair and tugged in frustration, growling softly. How could Urho be so obtuse? "Is it not serious, you fool? What you have isn't serious?"

"I have no idea *what* it is." Urho wiped a hand over his face. "I haven't seen him since he left for Virona. Between the twins, you, and this wretched flu season, I've barely had a moment, much less a day, away from the clinic or work. And he can't come here. He's 'banished' from the city, according to him. At least the work on his new office seems to satisfy him because otherwise, I'd worry."

"Jason talks to him."

"I talk to him, too," Urho said defensively.

Yes! This was what he wanted to know! This would be entertaining! Vale dropped his voice conspiratorially. "How often?"

"Daily," Urho admitted. His cheeks glowed.

"I see. So, it's not serious, but you talk every day, and you miss him. I can tell." Urho was such a fool. But Vale already knew that. He resisted rubbing his hands together eagerly.

"I didn't say it wasn't serious. I said it's complicated."

"You said you didn't know what it was."

"You're so exasperating today!" Urho started to stand, but Vale took hold of his shoulders and pressed him back down to the sofa.

"You have to tell me everything. Now."

"It's a long story, and it's been a long day."

Vale rolled his eyes. "I'm a miserably pregnant omega who is essentially trapped in this house by the flu epidemic and tortured daily by the attentions of my loving in-laws. *Please* talk to me."

Urho gave a quick half-smile and then cast a glance toward the liquor cabinet across the room. That was an excellent idea. The truth would come out of him more smoothly with a bit of bourbon.

"I'll pour you a drink if you tell me how it all began." Vale crossed the room and lifted the bottle temptingly.

"I found out that he was involved..." Urho trailed off. "He was in a dangerous situation. So, I offered to fuck him, like a surrogate for an omega."

Vale almost choked laughing. That was...that was more than he'd expected to Urho to give. He almost whooped, but instead, after pouring a generous glass, he collapsed beside Urho on the sofa and passed the bourbon over with a grin. "I see."

Damn, he was good.

Urho sipped the bourbon before going on. "I didn't anticipate how that turned out."

"Oh, I imagine you didn't." Vale was utterly delighted. This was the most exciting thing he'd heard in weeks. Someone else's dramas were so much more entertaining than his own.

Urho rolled his shoulders and took another swallow. "I hadn't realized that it would become something so..."

"Different?"

"More."

Vale leaned back on the sofa, grinning, with his hand on his bulging stomach. "Ah, then you're still the idiot I've always known and loved."

"I wanted to believe that what I was offering was no different than helping an omega in heat, but in reality, it was nothing like that at all."

"It was forbidden," Vale supplied, the rush of the taboo thrilling him vicariously. "Which is definitely different."

"Yes, but—" Urho squirmed on the sofa like an embarrassed child. An odd look for a man of his size and muscle mass.

"But?" Vale prompted.

"He reminds me of Riki."

That was the last thing Vale had anticipated hearing. "I thought Riki was a paragon of gentleness and obedience. Something Xan is decidedly not."

"Riki was. No, Xan isn't like him in that way at all." Urho scrubbed a hand over his head. "I meant the way I feel about him reminds me of Riki. The way I react to his scent and the way I want to…"

Vale sat up straighter. "Yes?"

"The way I want to own him."

"Oh, dear friend," Vale whispered, putting a hand on Urho's shoulder. "I suppose that must have shocked your old-fashioned, traditional soul nearly to death."

"I keep telling you. I'm not old-fashioned. If anything should prove it and put a nail in that coffin, I'd think it would be this situation." Urho smiled wryly. "I admit I did lose my mind at first."

"After you'd…" Vale made a lewd gesture that meant "fucked."

Urho grimaced. "No. Before I made the offer to him, I was in a state—overwrought, afraid, and angry. I wanted to protect him and shake him. I wanted to…" He trailed off. "Once I settled on the idea of acting as a surrogate for him, everything seemed to click into place. I was able to make peace with it."

"Well, you always did have a hero kink," Vale said. "I think that was half your attraction for me."

"No." Urho shook his head in denial.

Vale wasn't going to argue with him about it. Well, not much. "Oh, maybe our relationship eventually became more than heroism to you. But at first, you were my surrogate during heats because you wanted to save me from ever being in a dangerous position again. And then we became lovers outside the heats…and, yes. I'll concede that was based more on friendship and fun than on heroism gone awry. But that was where it had started."

He knew Urho would leave that discussion behind, either because it was still painful for him, or because he knew it was fruitless to hash out. And he was right. Urho began speaking of Xan again. "It's wrong, though. Two alphas. It's against the Holy Book and the law. How do I reconcile that it feels so right?"

"I think you're smart enough to know the answer to that." Vale flicked him a harsh glance. "The laws and Holy Books are all about control. But hearts are wild things. They can't be controlled no matter how much those in power wish it."

The child growing in his belly was proof of that. No amount of control would have stopped Jason's love taking root inside of him. Somewhere, deep inside, he'd come to believe that what had happened was destined, just like their bond.

"It's an obstacle," Urho mused, his mind clearly still occupied by thoughts of Xan. "We can never truly be together."

"Plus, there's Caleb."

Urho chuckled. "Yes, Caleb. Who is strangely accepting of all this."

Vale nodded. "Contracted relationships aren't like *Érosgápe*. I'm sure he has his reasons for being content with the arrangement." He'd heard the rumors about Caleb. Omegas gossiped, and there was a lot of gossip about when it came to someone as beautiful as Caleb Riggs waiting as late as he did to contract.

Urho tilted his head. "You know."

"I know what?"

Urho cocked his head, and Vale widened his eyes, all innocence. He might listen to gossip and rumors, but he didn't spread them around himself. At least not very often.

"Caleb is special."

"I think he's a wonderful man and Xan is lucky to have him." Vale shifted back with a grunt, rubbing his stomach. "Good wolf-god above, this child! He never rests."

"When he's bigger, he'll have less room to move around. So, he'll slow down."

Vale frowned at his stomach, imagining the terror that would come when that happened. "Then I'll panic and rejoice every time he makes himself known. I've heard as much from Miner."

"Miner's driving you up a wall, is he?"

"They both are. They'd put me in a glass cage if they could and feed me only the freshest fruit and vegetables straight from golden tongs."

"Interesting image."

Vale sighed and rubbed his bulge again. "So, with all that out on the table, indulge me some more. What's the plan now? How will you proceed with this relationship—is that even the term for what you have? And how are you coping with all of this time apart?"

"I'm not sure. Making plans is difficult because his cousin, Janus, an alpha with a reputation for seducing contracted omegas, has been sent there to spy on Xan. Or so he believes."

"Oh, I can believe it." Vale rolled his eyes. "Xan's father is a controlling man from what I've seen and all I've heard." Memories of ugly behavior at various social functions flashed through his mind.

"Yes. Well, Xan wishes he could get away from Virona to meet me halfway in Montrew, but he's so busy with his work. And I'm busy here, of course. Plus, his father has put the kibosh on Xan traveling anywhere near the city during this flu epidemic, and his cousin is there to enforce it."

"Jason didn't tell me about that. What if you went up to see him for a few days?"

"He says even if I did find a way to get up there, we wouldn't have any time alone. Not with his cousin keeping such a close eye on him."

Vale scoffed. "You could be inconspicuous."

"Perhaps." Urho rubbed a hand over his forehead.

"Don't be such a coward."

"What?"

If Urho didn't make a move, then he was sure to lose Xan or talk himself out of pursuing a taboo relationship with him. For some reason he only vaguely understood as love for both of his friends, Vale didn't want that to happen. "Surely you could find someone to look after the omega who is pregnant with twins? And we could engage another doctor—just for a day or so. What's really stopping you?"

Urho's shoulders drew up. "This flu contagion is growing in proportions that frighten me. The omega expecting twins and his alpha have decided it's too risky to stay in town. They're heading west to Elinton for the rest of his pregnancy."

"Perfect." Vale snapped his fingers. "When they're gone, you should go up and stay with Xan."

"I could, but—"

At that moment, Jason entered with a stack of mail and a tray of tea. He looked adorably flustered, and Vale's heart went all gooey at the sight of him. Really, it was ridiculous, and yet he wouldn't change it for the world.

"The door was only the postman. He was coughing up a storm. Ugly wracking coughs. I'm not sure he shouldn't be home." Jason nodded at the envelopes. "Out in this cold weather with a cough like that, he'll catch his death, as my father would say. And all for a stack of junk mail and fliers."

"Go wash your hands," Urho said gruffly, standing up. "And burn that mail."

Jason paled and stared down at the offending papers like he held a murder weapon in his hands. "The flu."

"Do what I said," Urho commanded.

Jason fled the room, and an acidic taste flooded Vale's mouth. He didn't know what he'd do if something happened to Jason. "Do you think he'll get sick?"

"I hope not. For your sake. The real danger, though, is if *you* get sick."

That didn't mollify Vale in the least. "I heard rumors that this flu is bad enough that some young people are dying from it. A boy just last week—younger than Jason, healthy and hale, and then he was gone."

"I think the omega with twins has the right idea." Urho sighed. "I can host you at my country home."

Vale's eyes went wide. Memories of heats he'd shared with Urho in that quaint house filled his mind. He shook his head. "No, no."

Understanding instantly, Urho nodded his agreement. "What about the house at Seshwan-By-The-Sea? The one Jason's parents keep?"

"They're heading there for their anniversary in a few weeks, and to be dramatic, I'd rather die than be caged in a house with the two of them right now. They're as bad as Jason, only I don't adore them." Vale groaned, explaining more about Miner and Yule's constant presence.

When he finally drew to a close, Urho laughed uncomfortably. "I don't know what to say."

"I know!" Vale threw his hands up again. "I've been looking

forward to them leaving town just to get a break."

"Virona is three hours north of here by train."

Vale raised a brow and stroked his stomach. "And?"

"And Xan is always saying that the house is empty, and Caleb is lonely."

Vale pondered. "I don't know if Jason will agree. He barely lets me leave the house to walk to the market or—"

"With this flu going around, I want you to stop that immediately."

Vale waved off his worry, irritation welling again. "I haven't been in over a week. I'm going stir crazy here. The garden is dying, and the flowers are going, and I haven't written a decent poem since I got knocked up. Do babies suck out all your inspiration? Is there scientific evidence of that? Because I could contribute to the studies."

Jason walked back in, looking shaken. "I burned the mail in the fireplace in the reception room and washed my hands in hot water. Do you think that's good enough? Should I shower?" He started to turn and leave again. "I can shower!"

"You're fine." Urho gestured to the leather wing chair. "Sit down. We need to discuss this flu epidemic and the risk to this pregnancy and Vale."

Jason sat immediately, eyes like saucers, intent on whatever Urho suggested. There was a time when Jason resented Urho far too much to have ever looked at him like that. Vale thought they'd all three come a very long way.

"I forgot to remake Vale's tea," Jason said quietly. "Can this wait until I get that for him?"

"Never mind, darling," Vale said, his heart fluttering at the sweetness of his alpha's heart. "I'm past wanting it now."

"He's very finicky lately. Is that normal?" Jason asked, looking to Urho for answers.

"Quite normal. Now, please listen. I was just telling Vale about the flu this season. It's ramping up, becoming an epidemic very quickly. Normally, I'd want to be here, in the thick of it, helping those who contract it. But I'm committed to Vale's health and dealing with whatever potentials come from this pregnancy. I won't put him in another doctor's hands. Which brings me to my suggestion—I think we should all three leave town."

"And go where?" Jason asked.

"Somewhere the flu hasn't reached yet. The sea, perhaps," Urho said. Vale almost laughed at the eagerness in his tone.

"My parents are already going to the cottage," Jason said, repeating Vale's comment from earlier. "Vale can barely stand their nightly visits. I don't think he'd want to be stuck with them in—"

"We can go to Xan's house in Virona," Vale interrupted. "He's invited us, hasn't he?"

"Well, yes, for the Autumn Nights feasts, but we declined, of course."

"Don't you think the offer probably still stands? Even though the feasts are passed?" Vale pushed, already thinking of how nice it would be to give birth by the sea, and how lovely it would be to have an omega friend at hand, too. Someone who wasn't his pater-in-law.

"I'm sure it does," Jason agreed. "He's always complaining that the house is so big and yet his cousin seems to be everywhere at once."

Vale interrogated Jason about the cousin, curious why Jason hadn't mentioned him much. Jason had been part of Xan's life since they were boys.

"He's a little older than us, but I never liked him." Jason shrugged. "Aside from that, I've had my mind on other things." His brows drew down. "Seeing Janus would be a negative toward going, but if push came to shove, we could always rent our own little place in Virona if we need to get out of Xan's hair."

"I want to be with Caleb," Vale said, clutching Jason's hand. "When the time comes, it would be good to have him there."

"I didn't know you felt so strongly for Caleb." Jason kissed Vale's knuckles.

"Omega brooding instinct," Urho offered in his gentle, doctor-knows-all tone. "They take solace in the presence of other omegas during their time. It's instinctual."

Vale gazed at Urho pointedly. "Or perhaps societal. And stop talking about me like I'm not here. Regardless, if Xan and Caleb will have us, then yes, I'm willing to go."

"You're coming, too?" Jason asked Urho.

"I made a promise to you both that I'd deliver this baby, and I will. So, if Xan will have me—"

Jason laughed. "Oh, he'll have you. This way and that."

Urho's cheeks grew darker. "Yes, well, then I'll be going, too."

"I think we just cinched our invite," Jason stage whispered in Vale's ear, eyes dancing.

Vale laughed, his restless, irritable mood lifting, if only momentarily. He'd give birth by the sea with the wind and the waves in the background, and with an omega friend by his side. Jason would loosen up there, away from the daily grind of work and taking care of Vale. And Vale would relax away from his in-laws. Urho would be with Xan, and this thing between them, whatever it was, would stand a chance.

Yes, this was a positively delicious idea.

CHAPTER THIRTEEN

"WHAT A TERRIBLE idea!" Father cried, his knuckles turning white around his fork and knife.

Pater, for his part, simply looked down at his plate.

Jason hated the sadness that slumped his shoulders, but he also knew he had to protect Vale and their child, more than he needed to protect his parents' feelings. "It's decided," he said firmly.

"But your pater wanted to be there when—"

Jason shook his head. "I realize that, but Vale and I have made up our minds to visit Xan and Caleb."

"There's room at Seshwan—" Father started, but Pater put his hand on his arm and silenced him.

"We understand," Pater said softly. "If Vale wants to be in Virona, he should be in Virona."

"We can also go to Virona," Father said.

"No," Jason interjected. "This is…we need…look, Pater, Father, the thing is—"

"You stay at Seshwan-by-the-Sea until the worst of the flu has passed," Vale interrupted. "Traveling to and fro between cities, and back and forth between Xan's house and town, will only increase the risk of exposure."

Pater flashed Father a hard look, and Jason wasn't surprised when his father stayed silent in the face of it. "If you wanted us to leave you be," Pater said, "all you had to do was ask."

Vale stilled, his fork hovering over his plate. "I didn't want to hurt you."

Pater shrugged. "Darling, what don't I understand about overbearing in-laws? If only Yule's had lived long enough to meet you. I'm sure we've been a bit much."

Father worked his mouth like he might protest, but then he didn't, choosing to swallow half of his glass of wine instead.

"We've been excited. Too excited, I'm sure."

"No," Vale said, and if the paleness of his cheek was any indication, he was feeling pretty guilty at the moment. "Not too excited."

"Father, Pater," Jason interceded. "We love you both, and we're happy that you're excited. We want you to be excited. Right now, Vale and I need some time alone—"

"In a house full of people in Virona," Father muttered.

"—alone in the way and place that we choose. Vale needs a place where he can relax and be taken care of, well away from the virus. I believe Xan's house in Virona is the perfect place for that. There are beta servants to handle his every need and Urho will be staying there with us."

"When I was pregnant with you," Miner said, plucking up his wine glass and taking a sip of the ruby red liquid. "I dreamed of giving birth at Seshwan-by-the-Sea, but Yule's pater wouldn't hear of it. And the medical services weren't very good in that area, and I was, of course, high risk..." He smiled, and though his eyes remained slightly hurt and sad, Jason thought he genuinely meant what he said next. "I wish you the birth of your dreams, in the place you are most comfortable, with Jason by your side." He lifted his glass for a toast, and even Yule lifted his, too.

After dinner, Jason stood with a glass of bourbon by the big windows in the study, looking out at the shadowy, moonlit garden. He made mental plans about what team of beta workers to hire and what instructions to give them in order to be willing to leave his beloved space in someone else's hands.

Pater sat with Vale on the sofa with his hands on Vale's stomach. Every once in a while, a subdued exclamation rose up. Evidently the baby was kicking very hard. A good sign, Urho said. Painful, Vale usually claimed. Warm affection filled Jason's chest as he turned back to the scene in the room.

His father stood by the fire, his drink on the mantle and a fond smile on his face as he watched Pater and Vale together. As for Vale, he was incredibly tolerant, almost sweet, to Pater now that they'd broken his heart with their announcement. His sweet omega might be cranky lately, but he was loving, and Jason was grateful to him for letting Pater touch and feel, exclaim and love.

Because Pater did love them both—all—passionately, and so did Father.

Jason stepped across the brick floor to join his father by the fire. "You understand, don't you?" he asked quietly, hoping only his father heard him.

"Of course, I do."

"It's what he needs."

Father nodded, picked up his glass, and took a swallow. "Don't worry. We aren't angry. The hurt will pass. It's natural. You're making your own family. It needs to be on your terms. Your way."

"I love you. We both love you," Jason assured him.

"Of course, you do." He sighed and tilted his head back, gazing up at the ceiling for a moment, before he brought his chin down again and gazed at the omegas on the sofa. "I wish I'd had your balls when I was your age. I wish I'd told my pater and father to back off. It pains me to think he didn't get the birth he wanted with you. I had hope that there would be another but…" He shook his head. "I never should have assumed. This is your precious one and only chance, Jason. We know that. Make it what he needs. Give him the birth of his dreams."

Jason scoffed. "From what I understand, the birth itself is hideously painful. I doubt there will be anything dreamy about it."

"No, but the end of his pregnancy will be special. Cherish it."

"I'll try."

"Don't let your fear swallow your joy."

Then, before Jason could reply, Father broke away and went to the sofa. "Move aside," he said to Pater. "I'd like to feel him once more tonight, if you don't mind, Vale?"

"Please do," Vale said, letting Father take Pater's place next to him. Pater lingered, his hands going to Father's shoulders and slipping into his hair. Vale took Pater's hand and placed it against the side of his stomach. "Just wait. It sometimes takes a—well, not this time."

Father grinned. "That was a healthy kick."

"He's strong. Urho says he's growing well."

Father murmured softly, "We'll be excited to meet him. Don't linger too long in Virona after he comes."

"But don't return before the flu is past us," Pater warned.

"We won't," Jason said to both of them. "We'll be safe, but we can't wait for you to meet him either."

"We love you," Vale said, his cheeks over his dark beard flushing. "You'll be wonderful grandparents."

The night ended earlier than usual, and Pater clung to Vale with an extra-long hug before slipping on his coat and following Father into the night.

"That went better than I expected," Jason said, wrapping his arms around Vale as they watched from the front porch. His parents got into their car where they had parked it by the sidewalk, and the engine turned over.

"Yes, but I still feel like an absolute asshole," Vale said. "Depriving them of this."

"No," Jason said. "This is what we needed to do. Come on. Let's feed Zephyr, and then up to bed. I need to massage your feet. Your ankles look swollen."

PART THREE

SEA BIRTH

CHAPTER FOURTEEN

VALE APPRECIATED THE hired driver's attempt to avoid the potholes on the ride from the train station to Xan's house by the seaside. But given the extra amount of time it seemed to take, he wasn't certain he wasn't going to get carsick before their journey's end.

Zephyr hissed in the carrier at their feet, and Jason was tense with eagerness to see his friend. Urho…well, Urho was tense with eagerness, too. Vale could only hope that whatever had finally ignited between his best friend and Jason's could be tended into a steady flame, and not explode into a disaster.

The baby had taken to performing gymnastics, using Vale's organs to kick off into contortions, and Vale was weary beyond the telling of it. Still Urho guaranteed him that the baby, once born, would be so cute that Vale would forget his irritation with it now. He believed it was true, but it didn't make a kick to the kidney feel any better.

"It's not far now," Jason said, putting his hand on Vale's stomach, and kissing his cheek. "Should I open the window?"

"Yes."

The sea air poured into the carriage with a salty wildness that gave Vale the shivers. He took deep, fortifying breaths, finding it settled his stomach and cooled his hot skin. "That's better," he murmured, wiping a hand over his beard. "Not much farther now?"

"Just a few more miles," the beta driver said, pointing ahead toward the sea cliffs. "The Lofton House is just that'a'way. What are you'uns doin' up at the big house?"

Urho pleasantly explained that the flu epidemic had taken off in the city beyond their willingness to risk exposure, and so they'd packed for a few months stay and trundled off together to their friends' home in Virona.

"Ah, yes, we're still blessedly free of the cursed sickness," the driver said. "So, are you gonna vacation the whole time then? Must be nice."

"No," Urho explained. "I'm a doctor, and Jason here is a scientist."

Jason scoffed and explained that he'd had to give up his work in the labs for the duration of the stay. But his work for his father's company could, sadly, be done from afar, and so he would still be occupied with it for several hours a day.

"Idleness is wolf-god's enemy," the driver said and rolled down his window to spit out. "Good thinkin' stayin' busy-like."

Vale didn't know that he agreed. He didn't want Jason working too much. It kept him from fulfilling Vale's every whim. Not that Vale wanted him unoccupied, per se. *That* would lead to nothing but indulgence in copious amounts of sex, and as horny as the pregnancy made Vale, it also made him irritable, too. He was well and truly sick of being fisted. Blow jobs? Great. Nipple play? Fantastic. Rimming? Please. But he wanted Jason's hand away from his asshole for the foreseeable future.

Yet, Urho refused to alter his prescription of a daily fist, and, in the heat of the moment, Vale never could resist that beautiful feeling of fullness, resorting to begging for it even. But for some reason, it left him annoyed later. It was too much and never quite enough. And he tended to get snappish afterward.

So maybe it *was* best if Jason worked at least part of the day.

Vale was sick to death of his own fickle company—one minute he wanted nothing more than to nap, the next he had to walk. One moment he wanted tea, and the next, he didn't. He craved fish, and then couldn't stomach it. He was cranky and anxious but didn't want Jason to share even a shred of his fear. Vale wished he could escape his head. He didn't know how Jason wasn't sick of being around him, as well.

"That must be it," Jason said, pointing at a large, red-roofed house as they bounced over a big pothole in the road.

The beta driver cursed and apologized. "The roads get rough in the spring rains, and no one's paid to fix 'em," he said.

The jolt made Vale's hips ache, and the scar tissue inside tightened like a rubber band. He hissed under his breath. Jason and Urho were annoyingly solicitous, and he bantered with them both briefly about the baby's chances of being adorable. High, Urho assured him. Jason simply nuzzled his neck and left Vale an annoyed puddle of goo.

Their destination, Lofton, loomed ahead and the chaos of their arrival was perhaps not as great as it could have been, but chaotic all the same. Xan and Jason greeted each other like pups, roughhousing in the yard like they were back at Mont Nessadare. And the electrical, lust-filled charge between Urho and Xan when they met again after months apart was enough to make Vale's omega glands swell with slick.

Caleb was a sight for sore eyes. Warm and knowing, he greeted Vale just the way he needed to be greeted—with affection and offers of food. Xan's omega was a calming balm, all blond and white and giving off a creamy glow that calmed Vale's nerves on sight. Urho claimed their immediate bond was due to a brooding instinct, claiming omegas are always drawn to one another for support during pregnancy, but Vale knew it was so much more than that.

Only another omega could ever understand what he now faced. No matter how much an alpha tried, he could not comprehend what it was to be subsumed by his body's demands. Omegas shared a commonality of surrender. During heat and pregnancy, they learned how little control they truly had over nature, and how little their egos mattered when it came to wolf-god's push for reproduction. That was something an alpha never understood, not even after the uncontrollable rush of an *Érosgápe* bonding.

That's why Caleb greeted him like a dear old friend, and Vale let the man ply him with soup and sandwiches before asking to be guided up to their room for a rest. Jason followed at his heels, and Caleb led them up a striking staircase that split at the top into separate wings of the house.

"The place is enormous," Caleb said with a sigh. "All the better to fill with babies, I suppose." This last he tacked on brightly, voice full of a cheerful hope that Vale recognized as Caleb's usual public persona. Frankly, he wondered how genuine the brightness really was, because, underneath, he sensed a kind of sadness that he couldn't quite put his finger on.

"Xan's family always did like to show off," Jason said, his hand on Vale's lower back as they took a left at the top of the stairs and then hung a right to walk a corridor decorated with rococo ornaments that seemed far from Caleb's personal style.

"Indeed," Caleb agreed.

The hallway boasted multiple bedrooms on one side and windows that opened to the courtyard below on the other. A breeze flowed in, cooling the air and leaving an imprint of sea-salt on Vale's tongue. He rather enjoyed it, and as the breeze curled through his hair, a deep relaxation began in his bones.

"This one." Caleb opened the room. "It has an en suite bathroom and a big bed. Urho will be just down the hall in a similar room. If you need anything—towels, fresh bedding, food at odd hours—don't hesitate to ask any of the servants, or to ring specifically for our man, Ren. He's sent from wolf-god above and never lets me down."

Vale hugged Caleb goodbye for the time being, and flopped back on the bed, his belly moving around beneath his shirt. Jason stood by the window, looking out, his shoulders stiff and his back straight. "Nice view?"

"A garden," Jason offered. "The servants seem to be wrangling it back into shape."

"Perhaps you can help them, darling."

"Maybe I will."

"The sea must be the other direction, then," Vale observed from his comfortable spot propped up by pillows. The bed was truly divine. The mattress had just the right amount of firm-but-soft to ease his aching body. Growing a baby was ridiculously hard, it seemed, and he didn't think omegas were given enough credit for the task. Too much was made of the miracle and not enough of the strife involved. He let out a low moan as the child shoved a foot into his rib and twisted it there.

"Are you all right?" Jason asked, immediately by his side, hands on his stomach to feel the baby move. "Should I get Urho?"

"You know I'm perfectly fine," Vale grumbled. "Just the usual aches and pains."

"The journey was more tiring for you than I realized it would be," Jason said, smoothing his hands over the bulge and then smiling when the baby kicked his palm with a sharp pop. "You need to rest."

Vale shrugged, not sure if he could sleep even if he tried. He was in that fretful state of exhaustion where he'd dearly love to nap but probably couldn't manage it. "I don't think I can." He moved to rise. "Maybe a walk in those gardens will help."

"No," Jason said firmly. "You will rest." He pushed Vale back down on the pillows and sat beside him. Minutes ticked by.

Vale sighed and muttered, "At least hand me my notebook."

Jason looked as if he might protest, but then he pulled the pencil and pad from Vale's luggage, brought up while they'd eaten soup by the servants. He handed it over.

Vale pressed the pencil against his lip, tapping it there, waiting for a flow of words to come. He hadn't written poetry in months. The font had dried up. All his creative energy went to the child inside. And yet he refused to give up. He had so many things he wanted to share with the world—the experience of pregnancy just one of them—and yet no words came.

Jason interrupted his not-writing with a question. "What do you think Xan and Urho are doing?"

Vale arched a brow. "You know exactly what they're doing, darling."

Jason cocked his head, considering, before rising to go look out at the gardens again. "Do you think we ought to feel jealous?"

Vale scoffed, tucking the pencil in the notebook and setting it on the night table by the bed. "Of Xan? And Urho?"

"Well, they were *our* lovers first. Before they were each other's, I mean."

Vale laughed and then laughed some more. He laughed until tears rolled down his face, and Jason started laughing, too. He came to the bed and wiped at Vale's wet eyes with the sleeve of his shirt. "Stop, stop," Vale said, half-heartedly pushing his hand away. "You're going to give me the hiccups making me laugh like this."

"I was serious," Jason said, still giggling, too.

"Jealous of them? Because we had them first?" Vale said, and his laughter returned until he finally let out a long breath, clearly trying to get a hold of himself. "No, darling. I don't think we should be jealous."

Jason nodded thoughtfully, his own laughter still tugging at his lips. "I know. It's just…it's strange isn't it? To think of what we used to do with them, and then to think they're doing that together. Right now, most likely."

"Not really," Vale said. "I just hope they enjoy it. They've both been pining long enough. If the act doesn't measure up to expectations, we could be looking at a long, awkward stay until this one makes his appearance." He touched his stomach then. The laughter seemed to have startled the baby enough to calm it. Vale had the sense the babe had paused mid-gymnastics to listen.

"They'll enjoy it," Jason said quietly. "Sexually, Xan is…"

Vale's eyes narrowed. "Careful, baby alpha. Don't make me kill your best friend in his sleep."

Jason laughed again. "So, you are jealous."

"Not of Urho, and not of Urho having him. Of him having once had you…" Vale shrugged. He'd taken Jason and Xan's former relationship with more ease than many *Érosgápe* would have, but he didn't like to imagine the details of it.

Jason shrugged. "He's easy to please, that's all I was going to say. I promise."

"Easy to please," Vale huffed, irritation flaring. "I don't recall making you work especially hard to please me either."

Jason laughed again and then sat on the bed, leaning close to nuzzle Vale's neck. "That could be a fun game. Want to play?"

Vale tried to pretend disinterest, but it lasted all of five seconds before his cock had betrayed him by creating a bulge in the front of his soft, drawstring maternity pants. "What are the rules?" he asked instead.

"I have to please you, and you have to make me work for it."

Vale smirked. "Oh, I see. Feeling the need for a little discipline, are you?"

Jason shrugged this time. "Maybe. It's just something we haven't done before. Not since we were courting anyway. Back then, I wanted to please you so desperately, but you acted like you weren't sure…" He licked his lips, eyes going shy and hot at the same time. "Like you weren't sure I was good enough."

"Oh, baby alpha, did I make you suffer very much?"

"Yes."

Vale smirked. "What if I still don't know if you have what it takes to be my man?" He went on with a hint of real sorrow in his tone. "What will you do about that?"

Jason growled softly and pushed him back into the mattress, slinging a leg over his thighs, and wrapping his arms around Vale's shoulders. Vale could tell that if it weren't for the baby, Jason would have flung himself on top of Vale and started ripping his clothes off. The babe required some measure of caution.

"Go on, then. Prove yourself," Vale ordered casually. He yawned. "I'll let you know if I'm impressed. Maybe you can earn the right to be my alpha."

Jason made short work of Vale's clothes and his own, and soon Vale was sweating and shaking as Jason sucked, licked, kissed, and fucked him to orgasm, and then did it again, and again. Despite the evidence of his pleasure, Vale pretended disinterest and uncertainty, causing Jason to redouble his efforts time and again.

Outside the window, Vale did not doubt the beta workers Jason had spotted in the garden below heard Vale's cries of pleasure, and he didn't care. Jason "earning his place" as Vale's alpha was sheer bliss, and he had no reason to hide how lucky he was to be this man's omega.

As he came apart again—this time around Jason's thick cock—he threw back his head and granted Jason the reprieve he'd earned. "You're mine," Vale gasped. "My alpha. Mine alone."

Jason roared as he came, clutching Vale's shoulders as he took him from behind, and crying out his pleasure. Floating back to earth, Vale smirked. No doubt somewhere in the house Xan and Urho were having their fun, too. But there was no way what they shared could compare to his joy in Jason.

CHAPTER FIFTEEN

Three weeks later

THE SEA WAS alive. Jason could think of no other way to describe the sense he got when he stood next to it, staring out at the thrashing water. It was beautiful, yes, but wildly so. The Virona ocean was much less tranquil than the water by his parents' cottage at Seshwan-by-the-Sea. It was frothy and urgent. It should frighten him.

And yet it was the only place he wanted to be.

Vale enjoyed it, too. His hours on the beach were the only times, outside of sex, when he didn't complain about his various aches and pains. As the child grew, the pressure on his scars became nearly unbearable, and Jason's ability to handle Vale's distress lessened by the hour. Still, he held it together, being the alpha. He hadn't allowed himself to cry since Urho had told him to get it together. Instead, he buried his fears as far inside as possible and presented nothing but confidence to his beloved. It took its own kind of toll.

At least he had Urho to talk with about it. Sometimes.

Urho had his own troubles. Xan was a handful, and Urho was busy trying to hold on to him.

"Look at the gulls," Vale said quietly, pointing toward the sky. "They swoop like they're spelling out words." He frowned. "That's almost good enough for a poem, but not quite."

Jason brushed his fingers over Vale's beard and into his hair, saying nothing. Vale's inability to write was one in a long list of regular complaints. He'd stopped trying to placate him and resorted to simply listening.

"I wish we could swim. Just think how the water would take the weight from my belly."

Jason said nothing still. There would be no swimming. The late autumn air was too cool and the water too frigid to even think it. But bundled up in sweaters, they could happily bask in the dull sun every day. The salty air and crashing white noise of the waves seemed to bring Vale and the baby a kind of peace that they lacked elsewhere. And Jason loved to sit with him, Vale's head on Jason's knee, both of them nestled between layers of blankets to stay warm.

"It's a war in there," Vale had said that morning before they'd set out to the ocean. "He's determined to beat me up from the inside."

Jason hoped there was no truth to the old omega's tale that the relationship between the babe and omega during pregnancy signified their relationship for the rest of their lives. Because Vale seemed to alternately adore the baby and resent it—first for stealing his words, and then for the ongoing pain he caused as he grew and moved. What if, in the end, Vale and the child didn't get along? Just look at Xan and his parents. There was no guarantee that they would all like each other.

Love each other, certainly. But like was another matter. Everyone knew that.

"I miss my pater," Vale said suddenly, sitting up as a wave crashed onto the shore, washing up a small raft of seaweed and a branch. "I wish he were here to tell me it was all going to be all right."

Jason rubbed Vale's back and didn't offer up much else. He'd never met Vale's parents, and while he'd been curious about them, Vale hadn't ever talked about them all that much. Not even when they'd discussed the cabin before renovating it. Not even when they'd walked around the property that day before the snowstorm.

"My pater was smart."

"I'm sure he was."

Vale shrugged. "My father was smart, too, of course, but he was the silly one. Joking and laughing all the time. Pater was serious as a heart attack. That's why I'd want him here to say that we're going to be all right. I'd believe him."

"If he were that serious, then he probably wouldn't say it at all."

Vale huffed. "No, he probably wouldn't."

"I wish he were here, too," Jason finally said. "I wish I'd known them both."

Vale smiled. "They loved each other very much."

"And you."

"Yes, they loved me, too." Vale touched his stomach. "We'll love him, Jason. Don't worry."

"I'm not worried about that."

Vale sighed. "I know you are. That old omega tale has wormed under your skin. But there's nothing this one can do that will make me not love him. Even if he kicks my spleen out while he's in here."

Jason nodded and kept his thoughts to himself. He could think of one thing the babe might do that could make him not love it. If Vale didn't survive then Jason wasn't sure how he'd ever forgive himself...or the baby.

The sun was falling in the sky, and it was time to get Vale back up to the house. "Dinner will be served soon."

Vale sighed and let Jason pull him to his feet. "How was your time in the gardens?"

Jason smiled, putting his hand on Vale's back and taking his arm to guide him toward the stairs that led up to the house. "It was good. The gardener has finally accepted that I don't want to meddle, just help."

"He's lucky to have you."

"I'm lucky he didn't quit when I first showed up. That would have left Caleb in a mess."

"Caleb would manage. I get the impression he always does." He started toward the house, one hand on his stomach, and the other in Jason's grasp.

Vale waddled more and more every day, and Jason kept close to him. Especially on the way to and from the beach. The dunes, the stairs, and even the sand itself could shift about under Vale's feet and leave him tipping over.

"Did you talk to your father?" Vale asked as they reached the safety of the path near the gardens.

"Yes."

"And he's not angry?"

"He understands."

Vale nodded knowingly. "They're *Érosgápe*. Of course, he does."

Jason's work for Sabel Enterprises had been handed off to another employee when his father realized that he was too distracted by Vale's needs to handle it properly. He felt guilty about that, certain that a better alpha would have been able to do both, but he wasn't willing to risk a single moment with Vale for something as mundane as car parts. Not when he wasn't sure Vale would make it through the pregnancy, much less the birth.

No amount of Urho's assurances and Vale's apparent robust health could take away the dagger of fear lodged in Jason's heart. Nor could it stop his mind from interpreting every whimper and moan as evidence that Vale's body wasn't going to weather this storm. But he had to keep it all locked down.

Pushed deep.

No leak of his true fear was allowed. Vale needed Jason's belief as much as he needed food and water. So, he'd fake it until they had a crying, healthy baby in their arms, and Vale was assessed as safe, too. Then, maybe, he'd let himself fall apart with relief.

"This is taking longer than I imagined," Vale said, as Jason scurried ahead on the path to open the door for him. "I never realized that, aside from the pain, being pregnant could be so dull."

Jason wished he found it dull, too. Unfortunately, he still found it terrifying.

CHAPTER SIXTEEN

A month later

THE RELIEF IN the house was palpable. Catching, even, in its pleasant strength.

The relationship between Xan and Urho was flourishing to everyone's satisfaction and delight. Caleb's printing press and supplies had been delivered, leaving him happily creating all day and buzzing with cheerfulness at night. And Janus, Xan's cousin who had been staying with them at Lofton to act as a spy for Xan's father, had been summoned away from the house for a spell, and everyone felt the joy of his absence.

Vale saw the relief in Jason, too. His gait was easier, more re-laxed, and his smile came brighter as the days passed. Vale suspected it was less to do with the absence of Xan's annoying cousin, and more to do with the progress of Vale's pregnancy.

"His pulse is lower, and his blood pressure is down," Urho said. He put his stethoscope and the portable blood pressure cuff back in his black doctor's bag and sat back on his heels.

Vale was propped up on pillows on the sofa in the library, a half-dozen partially-read books spread out along the length of the cushion. Urho was at Vale's feet for the examination, and Jason stood behind the sofa, hands on Vale's shoulders as he kept an eye on the proceedings.

Urho placed his palms against Vale's ever-growing bulge and pressed gently, making sounds beneath his breath.

"Well?" Jason asked.

Vale smirked. Oh, his adorable baby alpha—always so impatient.

"The babe seems to be the right size."

"Why are we doing this here?" Jason asked. "You can't examine his scars in public like this."

"Oh? I believe you've been 'examining him' in nearly every empty room of this house lately. And, rumor has it, even the garden," Urho said with an eye roll.

Vale laughed. He and Jason were never going to live down the last month. They'd been busted multiple times, in multiple places, by far too many people in mid-lovemaking. But Vale wasn't ashamed. He was pregnant for the only time in his life, and he was going to fully and completely enjoy the only part of it that wasn't painful or dull—copious amounts of sex.

Jason, though, tightened his grip on Vale's shoulders and growled softly. "You're not examining him in here."

"No, I never planned to," Urho said, sitting back on his heels again. "He's fine."

"How can you be sure?"

"I examined him yesterday. He was well-stretched, loose, and on track for a healthy birth. He won't have tightened up again overnight. Especially since I heard the evidence of your stretching him wide last night."

"Stop embarrassing him," Vale said, choking on a laugh.

"I'm not embarrassed," Jason said roughly. "I'm proud of what I do to you. And how well I do it."

Vale flicked a brow up and smiled amusedly down at Urho. "Indeed. You are very good at it."

"Ugh." Urho rose to his feet. "The babe is healthy, Vale is healthy, and so far, this pregnancy has been a miracle. Let's hope that holds." He slapped his hands together. "Now, if you'll excuse me. Xan and I have plans in town."

"A date?"

Urho smiled smugly but said no more.

Vale saw the stress lift from Jason's shoulders as Urho exited the library, leaving them together. "Did you hear him?" Jason said with relief. "He said you're on track for a healthy birth. I should call my parents. Let them know the good news."

Vale grabbed Jason's hand and tugged him down beside him, quickly shoving away the books so that they wouldn't get crushed by his handsome, firm butt. Vale almost laughed again, already feeling his arousal sharpen at just the thought of Jason's ass. He was far too easy these days. Always ready to be transported into pleasure. Still, there were a few things to address first before he could indulge another orgasm.

"Darling," Vale said, slipping his fingers through the flop of blond hair on Jason's forehead, pushing it aside. "I love how you've grown so alpha and valiant as the pregnancy has gone on, but there are a few things we should discuss."

"Such as?"

"Well, last night at the dinner table, for example."

Jason's chin went up.

Ah, so he knew exactly what Vale was referring to then. All the better.

"Did you need to *growl* at Xan over the cut of meat? There's always good meat at the Heelies-Riggs table. More than enough to go around."

"But you deserve the best slice," Jason argued. "You're growing a baby. You need the nutrients more than they do."

"You're so sweet, darling, but the remaining pieces were perfectly acceptable. You didn't need to scare the meat off Xan's plate and onto mine."

Jason shrugged, unrepentant.

Luckily their friends had found Jason's behavior amusing, but it wasn't polite all the same.

Jason said, "It's my duty to make sure you're well-fed and provided for."

"You already do! You bring me fresh fruit, obtained from I don't know where this time of year, and make sure I drink plenty of water. You don't need to scold our friends into providing for me, too." Vale couldn't help but tease. "Do you want Xan giving me massages at night, too?"

Jason snarled lightly. "I think not."

"Exactly. Let's not impose on our friends more than we already have by staying for months in their house. If Xan wants the best cut of meat in his own home, then let him have it."

"I'll consider it," Jason said a little sulkily, and Vale almost laughed again. His alpha was so determined, so anxious to please.

Jason tried to protect Vale from everything that might bother him, like sobering news from the city, phone calls from Miner and Yule, and even Zephyr, who'd been more of a problem than Vale had anticipated when he'd insisted on bringing him.

"Darling, about Zephyr," Vale said with a hint of frustration.

Jason hastened to assure him. "I'm sure it won't happen again."

"It's happened twice."

"She's just trying to be helpful."

Vale smiled gently. Obviously, Jason could relate a little too well to Zephyr's need to contribute. "Still, the mess both times was beyond gruesome."

"I cleaned it up."

Vale cocked a brow again.

"I helped the servants clean it up," Jason said. "She's bringing you gifts, helpful meals for her pregnant pater."

"But it's wholly unappreciated by him," Vale said with a shudder, remembering the dead mouse on his pillow and the dead bird the following night. Both times, Jason had summoned servants to deal with it and assisted them with the gore with barely a grumble, all while Vale sat by in a chair and tried not to weep with horrified laughter.

"What do you think we ought to do about her?" Jason asked.

"I think we need to bar her from the bedrooms for the time being. Urho says the germs from the kills alone could be detrimental to my—"

That was as far as he got before Jason rose from the sofa again, calling for Ren, Xan's butler, and requesting the door to their bedroom always be kept closed, rather than being left open after the servants had done their work within. Then he insisted that barriers be erected to keep Zephyr on the downstairs level, for the most part.

"Won't she just jump the barriers, sir?"

"Likely. But we shouldn't make it easy for her to drop dead animals on our beds."

"Too true."

It was delightful to hear Jason speak his orders so concisely and firmly with no margin for misunderstanding.

Shivering, Vale's asshole released slick, and he chewed on his bottom lip, anxious now for Ren to go away, so he could convince Jason that the library might not be a good place for a medical examination, but here, on the sofa with the books, was the perfect place for a screw.

Ren left to do as he'd been told, and Jason turned to Vale with glowing, hot eyes. "I can smell you opening for me."

"Always," Vale said, his voice husky. "I need you, darling. Please."

Jason didn't need to be asked twice. As soon as the door shut on Ren's retreating back, he put Vale on his knees, hands on the back of the sofa, and tugged his soft, drawstring pants down around his knees. There was no preparation. No need for it these days. Jason unbuckled his pants and pushed in deep, his cock rubbing against his swollen glands, and setting Vale off immediately.

The first orgasm took Vale's breath away.

But the third was so stunning, Vale was sure his shouts startled the servants.

By the sixth, they were both in another world, lost in each other and the pleasure they built and released between them. Two *Érosgápe,* blissed out on their bond. Deeply in love and growing a baby.

CHAPTER SEVENTEEN

J ASON HAD ALWAYS adored mucking around in the dirt, helping
things to grow. The way he'd put Vale's back garden to rights
had turned them into the envy of the neighborhood in summers,
and it always looked lovely in winter, too. Vale knew that abandon-
ing it for this trip to the sea for the duration of the pregnancy had
been a loss to Jason's sense of self. So, it was lovely to see him down
on his knees, grinning, as he pulled up weeds and used a small hand
trowel to dig holes for the plants the gardener passed to him.

In the spirit of support, as the autumn lengthened into a mild
winter, Vale bundled up and sat on a bench in the garden with a
book to read and watch Jason help put in cold-weather flowers. He
loved the songs the workers and Jason broke into and smiled
happily as they started in on an Old World tune he recognized as
his own pater's favorite.

All in all, the last few weeks had been good. The pains had even
lessened as the babe stopped growing as quickly. Urho said the baby
was busy adding his finishing touches now, which gave Vale's body
time to adjust and prepare for the birth.

A shadow blocked the sunlight to the page of Vale's book,
blocking out the poetry he'd taken to reading in lieu of writing his
own.

"For you, good sir," Jason said, sweeping into a bow. In his
outstretched hands, he held a handful of pink winter-blooming
heather. It smelled musky and lightly floral. "Your favorite winter
posy."

Vale took them from Jason and smiled as he dropped to his knees in the dirt before him, a goofy expression on his face. "What's gotten into you?"

"The mail truck arrived."

"So?"

Jason picked up Vale's free hand and kissed the knuckles. "Your hands are cold."

"I'm fine. Darling, what were you saying about the mail truck?"

Jason shrugged and then pointed toward the house. "Inside. Now."

"But…"

Jason raised a brow. "Don't dally. Do I need to use my alpha voice?"

Vale shivered. "It couldn't hurt."

Jason drew closer, going up on the balls of his feet to growl, "Get inside. I have plans for you."

Vale always enjoyed Jason's plans, especially since they usually involved sex, but they'd already fucked and fisted that morning. It seemed early to indulge again. "What plans?"

"Don't question your alpha."

Vale knew that tone and this game. It sent warmth flooding his groin. If he was cold before, he wasn't now. Still he resisted. "I was in the middle of this poem, darling, about apple trees in summer. Can't I finish it up before—"

Jason shook his head, tugged Vale up from the bench, and pointed at the house. "Up to our room. Clothes off. Robe on. I'll meet you there shortly. I just need to grab a few things first."

Vale frowned, not sure he wanted to be ordered about, but when Jason leaned close and whispered, "You'll do as I say," Vale shivered and nodded sharply. He would indeed.

Jason met him in their room as discussed, with a jar in one hand, a box under the other arm, a bag hitched over his shoulder, and a wicked grin on his face. "Good. You're ready. Perfect."

Vale was naked under his robe, and hard, of course. But he was confused when Jason sat down at the edge of the bed with all of his small burdens and opened the box to reveal a chocolate cake.

"What's going on?"

"It's your favorite."

"Chocolate layer cake, yes, I can see that."

"From Ellio's."

"In the city? You had it shipped from my favorite bakery in the *city*?"

Jason nodded. "Taste it."

Vale took the fork from Jason who'd withdrawn it from the bag he'd been carrying, along with a thermos of what smelled like coffee, and two cups. "We aren't going to slice it?"

"Be decadent."

With a quiver of expectant joy, Vale pushed his fork into the thick cake, taking a chunk from the top, and depositing the frosting-covered bite into his mouth with a whimper of delight.

"Don't eat it to the point of sickness," Jason said as Vale dug in. "I have other plans, and I don't want you queasy for them."

As soon as Vale sat back with a heavy sigh, Jason whisked the rest of the cake away to the table near the window. Turning back to Vale, he cracked open the jar that'd been sitting on the bed since he came in, releasing the scent of mint into the room.

"Take off your robe."

Vale obeyed and got comfortable on his back. "Now what?"

"Now I'll take care of you."

The massage began at his toes and Vale luxuriated in the cooling, minty lotion as Jason worked his way up, spreading Vale's legs to kneel between as he went. He worked the lotion into Vale's tender hips and thighs and skirted his genitals. Vale was relieved since the mint would burn uncomfortably on that sensitive skin.

Once Jason reached Vale's belly, he opened the robe, exposing Vale's flesh to the cooler air in the room. He paused for a moment, observing the baby shifting around inside restlessly, and his full lips stretched into a soft smile. Vale's chest grew hot with adoration. Then Jason scooped up extra lotion from the jar, and smoothed it over the hot, stretched skin of Vale's bulging abdomen. Vale moaned as the lotion cooled him down, making him shiver, and soothing where his body was stretching so quickly.

"You're beautiful like this," Jason murmured. "Full with our child." His fingers slipped all over Vale's stomach, rubbing and working the lotion in so that the tight skin sang with pleasure.

Vale shifted, his heart fluttering. "I'm huge."

"The most beautiful I've ever seen you."

Vale huffed. "You think that every morning, no matter what. *Érosgápe.* I know, because I feel the same way."

Jason kissed his stomach, laughing when he pulled away. "My lips tingle now."

"Don't get it in your eyes."

Jason lifted a brow as his hands slipped farther up over the mound of the baby and to Vale's chest. "How would it feel on these, I wonder?"

Vale bit his lower lip, and his cock woke quickly.

"Shall I try it?"

Vale moaned.

"I'll take that as a yes." Jason's hands slowly slid over Vale's ribs, up over his tattoo, and toward his nipples, giving him plenty of time to change his mind.

Vale's toes curled as Jason began to rub and play with his tender, milky nubs, and the usual flow began to slip down the sides of his chest toward the bed. Then the cold-hot sensation of the mint lotion kicked in, and the burn was divine. Vale groaned, tossing his head back, and spreading his legs wide.

"Oh, baby, such a slut for me." Jason laughed, continuing to toy with Vale's nipples, and doing nothing to rid himself of the pants that prevented any sort of fucking from happening.

Vale lifted his knees with his hands, exposing himself as much as possible, his cock aching now, and his hole wet with slick. Jason just laughed and tortured him more, playing with his nipples, rubbing his belly, and whispering about all the things he was going to do, all the ways he'd make Vale come…

"That's right. Just like that," Jason murmured. "Look at you."

Vale hitched a sharp breath, his body clenching with pleasure as his sensitive nipples led him into his first climax. "Unfair," Vale gritted out, still shivering and wanting more. "You know I come easily like that."

"You come easily always," Jason said, still laughing. "If I jerked off in your mouth, you'd come that way, too."

Vale knew he would. Omegas were blessed (or cursed, depending on the point of view) with multiple orgasmic capacities and triggers, and he wasn't known for fighting or delaying his pleasure. "But I want you inside me," Vale whispered. "I need it. Help me, alpha. Fuck your omega. Please."

"Mmm, you're so sweet when you beg," Jason said.

But he pulled away, sitting back on his heels, his pants bulging with arousal, but no intention, it seemed, of fulfilling Vale's demands. His eyes took on a gleam that made Vale growl and release his legs in frustration.

"I have something else in my bag. Another fun thing from the city."

Vale narrowed his gaze, panting.

Jason pulled out a fat, thick anal plug, and showed it to him. It had a pump attached, and when Jason demonstrated, Vale blinked rapidly. The plug swelled up three times its regular size and boasted a fat knot at the base.

"The latest in heat helping toys," Jason said. "But good for stretching pregnant omegas' passages, too."

"Is that…safe? It won't hurt him?"

"It's more than safe. It's recommended." Jason stood then, going into the en suite bathroom with the plug to wash it and the mint lotion from his hands. He returned with a towel and their bottle of lube. Usually unnecessary because of the copious slick Vale produced, especially as the pregnancy progressed, but apparently, he wasn't taking any chances.

"Lift your legs again," Jason commanded, using his no-nonsense alpha voice. "That's right."

Vale's nipples were really starting to burn now, and he shivered as the rest of his body cooled from the peppermint lotion. He tingled and ached, and wanted, but he wasn't sure how he felt about the thick, black thing Jason showed him one more time before smothering it in lube.

"Deep breath."

If he was going to say no, he should do it now. He didn't. A curiosity started deep within him. Just how big would it feel inside? As big as Jason's knot during heat? And how would he like that kind of fullness now that he was so big with the baby, and without the heat pheromones to make him need that almost-pain of being so stretched?

"Let it out," Jason said, and as Vale released his breath, he pressed the thick plug in. The base of it rested outside his body, and the rest seemed to fill him already, what with the space inside so occupied by the babe. "Good?"

Vale nodded.

"That's right. Now, hang on." Jason rubbed the inside of Vale's thighs and then up to tweak his burning nipples. "That feel nice?"

Vale squirmed, and his cock pressed up against the hump of his belly. "Yes."

"Mm, it looks nice." He tweaked Vale's nipples again. "So red and milky."

The milk did soothe the burn a bit as it released, but not entirely. Vale spread his legs wider, arousal burning in his groin, and he whispered, "I need you. Please."

Jason took the pump in his hand and then moved to lay down beside Vale. He turned onto his side, lifting up on one elbow, and then kissed him, fingers stroking his beard. "Ready?"

Vale shot him a glare. He'd been ready.

Jason laughed and then began to squeeze the ball to inflate the plug inside. At first, Vale felt nothing, but then the knot began to inflate, and he moaned, his prostate and omega glands being worked hard. "Oh," he whimpered. "That's…oh. Jason, darling, that's going to make me come."

Jason squeezed the pump faster, and Vale lost his first load all over his stomach as he convulsed in pleasure.

"Beautiful," Jason assessed. "More."

Vale barely had time to process that before Jason was stretching him even more, enough that his scars pulled taunt. "Ah, enough. Enough, darling."

"That hurts?"

"Yes."

"Too much?"

Vale struggled with wanting to say yes, knowing Jason would back it off, and rather enjoying the sensation of discomfort. It, along with his burning nipples, was just enough to keep his mind from wandering, and with a little more stimulation, he knew he'd shortly be transported to the place he most loved to go with Jason. "It's good, just no more."

"Does it feel like a knot?"

"Almost." It was too detached, and that overwhelming feeling of rightness was missing, but it was a good sensation—a strong one.

Vale could see how it would help in a heat to let a tired alpha rest. But it wouldn't be enough to hold off the need for a real knot for more than a wave or two.

Jason let the pump drop, and turned his attention to Vale's body, kneeling up next to him and running his hands over his entire form. He stroked over his shoulders and arms, his chest and sides, and spent extra time on his stomach—being tender and firm, stroking and loving it. He spread Vale's cum and pre-cum around and then brought it up to his mouth and licked it from his fingers. "Mm, a bit minty," he assessed.

Then his hands dipped lower to Vale's thighs again, and he moved to kneel between Vale's legs once more. "This is where it gets good, baby," he said.

Then he took Vale's hard cock into his mouth, reaching down to work the plug in his ass to the same rhythm as his bobbing head. It didn't take long after that for Vale to hit the heights where he rolled between orgasms, anal and penile, and was left a shaking, aching pile of flesh.

"Still hurt?" Jason asked, nudging the base of the plug.

Vale shook his head, eyes still rolled back, and a little drool at the corner of his mouth. He'd lost track of time, but he thought a good amount of time had passed while he writhed in ecstasy.

"I'm taking it out now," Jason said. The sensation of the plug deflating was odd. Much faster than when Jason's knot went down. The slide of the toy out of his passage left him feeling empty, but that only lasted a minute.

At some point, Jason had shoved his pants down around his hips, and he pushed inside quickly. Holding Vale's legs beneath the knee, he was able to get in deep. Over the curve of his stomach, Vale watched Jason pump into him. He was so beautiful, with his blond hair on his brow and his blue eyes burning hot over flushed cheeks. Vale shattered several more times on the demanding rod of

Jason's cock, until Jason groaned, coming hard, and tossing his head back with the force of his orgasm.

"Yes," Vale whispered. "Give it to me. I want it."

Jason shook and trembled, his hips jerking several more times, pegging Vale's glands, and they finally both eased down from the final climax. Pulling out, Jason collapsed beside Vale, taking his cheeks in hand, fingers stroking his beard tenderly, and kissed his mouth. "I love you," he whispered.

"I love chocolate cake," Vale replied, laughing. "And you. And him." He put his hand on his stomach, where the baby was now calm. Fucking always seemed to rock him to sleep.

"I can't wait to meet him," Jason said fondly, his hand falling to Vale's stomach. "He's going to look just like you."

"No, like you."

"I insist that he look like you."

Vale laughed and nuzzled Jason's cheek. "Baby alpha, if you have that kind of power, then I won't ever doubt another word you say."

"Then don't doubt this," Jason said, leaning up on an elbow to look Vale in the eye. "You're going to be fine. He's going to be healthy. We're going to be a healthy, happy family."

"Yes," Vale agreed. "I believe you."

Jason sighed and then sat up, flushed and sweaty still. "Well, I have to clean this up," he said, looking at the jar of lotion, the plug, the semen and slick everywhere, and the cake crumbs in the bed.

"Or we could eat more cake," Vale suggested, nodding toward the box on the table. "I'll even share this time."

Jason laughed and climbed out of bed to fetch the cake and fork. "You always have the right priorities."

"I do," Vale agreed.

You and this baby and a happy life. Nothing more. Nothing less.

And that, he knew, was everything.

CHAPTER EIGHTEEN

Three weeks later

THE HOUSE HAD descended into madness.

Or that's how it felt to Jason.

Xan's cousin Janus had returned from his visit to the city and brought back the flu. He was isolated from the rest of the house, but, from what Jason heard, Janus was sick enough to be on death's doorstep. And *now* Xan had abandoned them for the city to visit his ailing pater, leaving Urho a sad-sack mess, and Caleb strangely anxious.

And, as if wolf-god hadn't thought all that added quite enough spice to their placid seaside life, Jason was quite certain he was losing his mind. All afternoon he'd scented something delicious in the house. Something sensually delicious. And it was making his dick hard. If Vale, huge and restless, exhausted and cranky, saw him walking around with an inexplicable hard-on, he was going to be in a world of trouble.

At first, Jason thought it was simply something the chef was making for dinner.

And then he'd thought a Vironian omega had crept onto their property on the verge of going into heat. Probably looking for a wealthy alpha to seduce and catch a child with. And then it'd hit him…

Literally.

The scent wafting into his and Vale's room as Caleb walked by the open door, where Vale had been trying to nap, was undeniable.

That anxiety Caleb had been leaking since Xan had left? It'd coalesced into a very specific, arousing scent, and it meant only one thing—one very troublesome thing.

Vale let out a soft growl from his bed, peeling his eyes open. "Did you just get hard for another omega?"

Jason swallowed desperately. "Stay here. Don't move. I'm getting Urho."

"I'm *fine*."

Though Vale wasn't fine, they all knew it. He'd been having new, intense pains for the last several days, and the baby had shifted to a head-down position. Urho was plying Vale with the strongest muscle relaxants he could without injuring the babe, and yet the pains were growing more intense. He was barely sleeping at night and drowsing all day. Jason was doing the same. But they both knew the baby was coming soon. The issue was how soon and if it would survive.

Still, Jason soothed Vale, saying, "This isn't about you. Not this time."

"Touch that reeking omega and I will kill you both," Vale muttered darkly, propped up on pillows and barely able to move beneath the lump of the baby growing in his stomach. Jason almost asked just how he thought he'd manage that, but he couldn't bring himself to upset his omega any more than he already was. What was happening, and Jason's physical and pheromonal reaction to it, wasn't anyone's fault, but it was still a very big problem. And he could tell Vale was pissed as hell about it. Being aroused by another omega in front of a very pregnant *Érosgápe* was never a good look, and Jason needed someone, anyone to fix it.

"This can't be happening," Jason muttered, as he left Vale fairly crackling with barely repressed rage and rushed through the hall looking for Urho. "Not now. Not right now."

But there was no denying that he was hard as a rock, and it had nothing to do with Vale, and everything to do with the overwhelming scent Caleb was letting off. He reached Urho's bedroom door and shoved it open, finding Urho napping in his bed. He supposed he couldn't knock his friend for that, given his and Vale's tendency to sleep the days away as the babe grew bigger and bigger, and yet he was frustrated to find him napping at a crucial time like this.

"Urho, we have a problem."

Jason couldn't believe he had to spell it out to Urho. Even after Urho noticed the change in Jason's pheromones in reaction to the proximity of an omega in heat, he still didn't seem to get it. But when the realization finally took root, Urho leapt into action. He might be an uptight prig, but he could be counted on in an emergency, and there was no doubt this counted as one.

Especially since Vale started crying out in true agony not even ten minutes later.

VALE COULD SCENT the ripe omega in the house, and it infuriated him. Logically, he knew it was his friend Caleb, and deep inside, he felt sorry for what Caleb was going through. He knew him well enough now to understand why the arrangement between Xan and Urho worked so well for Caleb, too. But some other primal part of him viewed Caleb's heat, and the reaction it inevitably drew from all the alphas in the house, as a threat to his bond with Jason.

Beached like a whale in bed, he rolled onto his side, struggling for purchase on the sheets to stand up and follow to wherever Jason had disappeared. Jason claimed to be getting Urho, but Vale's exhausted, sleep-deprived mind was happy to supply him with all manner of visions, like Jason screwing a heat-addled Caleb up against a wall, while Caleb cried out for more, and begged for his knot.

Vale gnashed his teeth. He tried to roll off the bed, and instead froze, his stomach going rigid with a painful tension. He cried out, the contraction refusing to release. It amped up and up, scaring him until he was left moaning and panting as it finally let go. Sweat popped up at Vale's temples and in his armpits. He breathed in and out, trying to catch his breath.

Only a few minutes passed before the pain grabbed him again, and he yelled, loudly, trying to attract help from any direction. There were always beta servants around. And Jason…he needed Jason!

By the time the pain had released him again, Jason was there. "Baby? What's happening? Are you all right?"

Vale collapsed back on the bed, letting Jason's wild concern to wash over him. "Where were you?" he asked, leaning back on the pillows, panting from effort and feeling tense all over. "Did you go to him?"

"I was with Urho. He's going to deal with—"

Vale groaned and turned onto his side, his back and neck tensing, as he endured another contraction. They were coming fast, too fast from what he remembered. Pressure ground against his hips hard as the baby seemed to move inside him. "If you touched that omega—"

"You know I didn't. Don't be absurd," Jason said, his voice gruff and firm. "Look at me."

Vale looked over his shoulder, his breath still coming in sharply.

"Urho is going to handle it." Then his voice lost his alpha command, tipping up with concern and fear. "Are the pains worse? They seem worse."

Vale sighed as the contraction fled again, leaving him exhausted, but in no pain now. "I think…I don't know."

Jason went to open the window. The air from the gardens was cool and damp, and Vale took in big gulps of it, a strange foreboding washing over him. Closing his eyes, he lifted up a prayer to wolf-god, first for his baby, and then for himself, and then he met Jason's gaze again, seeing his own worry reflected there.

"I think the baby's coming," Vale said, slowly. "The pains are harder. Stronger than they've been. And…" He gasped as the overwhelming clutch gripped him. He shouted in agony.

Jason was up and running again before Vale could stop him. He was left reaching toward the doorway until suddenly one of the servants ducked his head inside. "Mr. Sabel is getting the doctor. He told me to tell you that it's going to be all right."

Vale gaped at him.

The man babbled on, "And I should know. My brother had a wee one last month, and it looked like it hurt somethin' awful, sounded like it, too by the shoutin', but they were both all right. You'll be all right, too."

Vale hauled himself from the bed, and the servant came rushing in to help him. "The window," he grunted. "Need some air."

Vale gripped the window frame, staring out at the garden as the pain came over him again. He was in the throes of it when Jason returned, his arm snaking around Vale to give him support. Jason nuzzled Vale's neck and whispered reassurances that barely made it past the white noise of pain and fear buzzing in Vale's head.

"You're going to be fine, baby," Jason said more firmly. "Do you hear me? Do you understand?"

Vale nodded. He did hear. And he understood, but what if…

Then Urho came into the room, reeking of Caleb's scent, and radiating frustration and worry. Urho dismissed the servant and Jason helped Vale lift his robe, exposing himself from the waist down for Urho to have a look. Vale clutched the windowpane as Urho knelt behind him and spread his ass apart to look. Another contraction came. By the time it had dissipated, Urho's examination and evaluation were conclusive—this was it.

The baby was on his way.

All the months of growing and hoping came to a head in clammy hands and grinding pain, but Jason was there, solid and certain, saying all the things Vale most wanted to hear, and suddenly found hard to believe.

"You can do this, Vale. You're going to be just fine. And the baby, too. I'm here. I've got you."

Vale whimpered, shaking his head until Jason took hold of his chin and insisted, "You will be all right. Say it."

"I will be all right."

"The baby is healthy."

"Yes, the baby is healthy," Vale agreed. Sweat slipped down his back, and he shivered as a cool breeze floated in the window.

"We're going to be a family soon. You and me and this one."

"A family—" Vale groaned as the pain took the rest of his sentence away.

Caleb's cries of heat-induced agony collided with Vale's shouts of pain. And as he labored by the window, refusing to get in the bed, the household dissolved into chaos and panic. Vale could hear it in the shouts from the hall, feel it in the strain Urho exhibited. In between contractions, Vale tried to collect himself, but it was all too much. It was all Vale could do not to panic, himself.

Jason was a rock, though. Calm and collected, putting Vale before any other distraction. He rubbed Vale's back soothingly, sang him lullabies, and held him in determined silence when the pains grew unbearable. His earnestness was so darling that it almost made Vale laugh. Except Vale was alternately in too much pain or too exhausted to laugh. He was scared, too, despite Jason's assurances. He was well and truly scared.

"I've got you," Jason said again. "You don't have to be afraid. I have you."

Vale looked into his blue eyes and took a deep breath, trying to believe, wanting to, and then when Jason took hold of his chin again and spoke in that deep alpha voice, it came home for him.

"You are my omega. Mine. You're strong enough to do this. And you will."

A flow of certainty started like a pinprick in Vale's doubt but soon flowed strong as Jason continued to encourage him. Yes, he would do this, and his son would be born, and they'd be a family. Just a little longer. Just a few more pushes.

After some more discussion and debate about moving to the bed—which Vale won again—Jason helped Vale put his leg up on a chair to give Urho more access to his birth canal. He wanted to remain standing. It felt right somehow to be on his feet. Lying down in a bed seemed all wrong.

Jason's face was pale but calm as blood and slick slipped down Vale's thighs onto the gathered towels. "You can do this," he reiterated. "I believe in you, Vale."

Vale nodded, a contraction coming on again, and he pushed hard.

"That's it!" Urho cried from where he kneeled at Vale's feet. "A little more. I can almost—"

"Help me!" Caleb screamed from the opposite wing. The words echoed around the massive house. Vale's memories of suffering an unserviced heat sliced through his current agony, and pity and rage tore through him at his friend's predicament.

"For wolf-god's sake, help him!" Vale shouted, nearly kicking Urho in the face where he knelt with his fingers in Vale's ass. Urho withdrew them quickly as Vale spun away from the window, glaring at him. "He's hurting. He's *suffering*. Go in there and help him."

"No!" Jason exclaimed, grabbing Vale by the shoulders. His face was flushed—his voice rough and certain. "We need Urho here. If something goes wro—" He bit off his words and added, "Vale, I can't deliver this baby. It's too risky. Urho stays with us until a doctor or our baby arrives."

"A doctor's coming," Urho said, standing up and obviously trying to sound as confident as he possibly could. "He should be here soon."

Vale wanted to argue, to remind them all that omegas gave birth every day and that he could do this. Jason had just said that he could, and he'd believed him! But then he groaned and held his stomach. He strained, eyes bulging as another contraction gripped his body, and he clutched the back of the chair with white knuckles to stay upright.

"That's it," Urho said. "Just breathe."

Vale sucked in a breath, and his entire body clenched. He screeched.

A matching, wrenching scream echoed through the halls and the still-open hallway door. Caleb's cries grew louder and louder as Vale's labor intensified.

The world was agony and he and Caleb were lost in it.

CHAPTER NINETEEN

J ASON'S MIND SPUN.

If Urho left them now to help Caleb and something went wrong with the birth, if the other doctor botched the job—assuming the other doctor even showed—he'd lose his *Érosgápe*.

But if Caleb were left to suffer, Vale would never forgive either of them. And neither would Xan, much less Caleb himself.

"Dr. Chase," Ren said suddenly from the doorway, a terror-filled expression on his face. Of course, there couldn't be any good news right now. Jason was starting to fear that the day was cursed. Ren raised a hand to cover his eyes at the sight of Vale's nakedness.

Jason snarled protectively but backed down when Urho put a hand on his chest. He turned his back on Ren, and instead focused on Vale, who was rocking through another contraction.

Ren's voice trembled as he explained why no one was coming to help them. "I got hold of Dr. Bainson in the village, and he can't make it. He's actually delivering another omega right now. He suggested I call Dr. Snid, an alpha doctor on the outskirts of town, but according to his omega, he's gone into the city to help with the flu epidemic."

"Fuck," Urho muttered, and Jason's heart galloped. If Urho was losing control, then he had every right to be scared. The optimism of the last few months felt as though it was circling the drain, replaced by cold, cold fear.

"Sir," Ren went on like he really didn't want to. "Mr. Janus is seizing now. His fever has gone too high for his body to hold. The cook is trying to cool him with cold water, but he's not respond-ing."

Jason didn't turn around, keeping his eyes and hands on Vale, but he felt nauseous. That didn't sound good. It didn't sound good at all.

Urho tore into his medical bag and brought out a bottle of medication, a syringe, and an empty hypodermic needle. "One syringe now. If he doesn't calm, then another in eight minutes." Urho returned to Jason and Vale's side. "I'm sorry. I know this isn't your job but—"

Another cry from Caleb's room rattled them all. Ren gasped, and Jason's heart squeezed. He met Urho's gaze, rocked to the core by the grim line of his mouth. Vale shouted as well. His body clenched all over as he held onto the back of the chair he'd had his foot on. Jason hushed him, but Vale was lost to him, gone deep into his pain. Eyes rolled back, Vale gritted his teeth and began to push. Jason stared as Vale's asshole bulged.

"Wolf-god!" Ren exclaimed in horror. He grabbed the medicine and syringe from Urho's hand and rushed away to administer the medication to Janus.

Adrenaline flooded Jason, leaving him feeling raw to the touch. He blinked in overawed shock as Urho knelt to the floor and spread Vale's ass cheeks wider, tugging the taut hole open enough to see a hint of something dark and fuzzy.

"Is the baby coming?" Jason asked, rubbing Vale's straining back and bending low to look. "Oh, wolf-god, is that his head?"

Urho shoved Jason aside. "Get out of the way."

Rage filled Jason, and unthinkingly he shoved Urho back with a snarl and growl. A need to protect his omega overriding rational thought.

Vale whimpered. "I will murder you both if you get into a fight right now. There is a baby coming out of me and—aaahhhh!" He howled, hunching again, his entire body going tense as he pushed harder, flushing all over.

"Yes, that's the head," Urho said grimly as slick rushed from Vale's asshole.

Another scream came from Caleb's wing, along with the sound of breaking wood. Then a violent thump. And another. Jason felt ill. Cold. Hot. Everything all at once. Sweat slipped down Jason's back, though nothing like the sweat flowing from Vale's body. His hands shook as he continued to rub Vale's haunches, and he stared at Vale's bulging asshole, breath held, waiting.

"What *the fuck* is going on?" a new voice snarled from the doorway.

Jason and Urho's heads whipped around to see Xan standing outside Vale's open door, his blue eyes dangerously narrowed, his curly hair a mess, and a large bruise on his cheekbone and another on his jaw. A combination of confusion and rage warred on Xan's face. "What the fuck is happening here?"

Vale gripped the chair hard and pushed again, wailing. The screams from Caleb's room came even louder.

Urgently, Urho turned to Jason. "Explain to him! I need to just…" Then he slipped a finger in beside the baby's head, and Vale shouted.

Instinct rose up hard, and Jason kicked Urho in the thigh. "Hurt him again, and I'll kill you."

"Stop!" Vale whimpered. "I can't… Let me… Oh, wolf-god, *fuck*!" He grimaced and pushed like some power greater than his own strength had hold of him. His hole opened enough to reveal a swath of the baby's brown-fuzzed head.

"Mr. Riggs is locked in, Mr. Heelies, sir," a beta servant from the hallway explained to Xan. "He's in heat."

"Well, don't just stand there—take me to him!" Xan barked.

Urho looked like he yearned to go to Xan and explain to him

what was happening, but things with the baby were moving too quickly. A rush of blood gushed down Vale's legs. Head spinning, Jason cried out in panic. Urho shoved him away hard.

The baby slipped out into Urho's hands. Perfect, whole, and covered with slick, mucous, and blood. The child let out a lusty scream. Jason stared at him in shock, and then Vale collapsed onto the chair, blood still coursing from his asshole. His beautiful hands reached out for the baby, and Jason blinked, staring at the umbilical cord that pulsed between them.

Jason's knees gave out then, and he found himself kneeling beside Vale as Urho passed off their blood-covered, plump, and screaming child to them. Vale took the sweet thing into his arms.

"Look, baby alpha. Look what we made."

Jason burst into tears. Vale kissed Jason's head, and then the baby's, and then Jason scented them both. All three of them huddled close, damp, slick, and full of emotions too raw to bear.

"I should feed him," Vale whispered. He tugged open his robe, placing the babe to his chest and cooing as the infant latched on and began to suckle.

Jason wiped tears from his eyes and kissed Vale's forehead. The moment was intimate and sweet, but Urho apparently had some work to do on Vale's insides. While they stared at their son, Urho convinced Vale to get into the bed with Jason and their baby, while Urho set about the work of making sure Vale would heal inside well.

Jason and Vale snuggled their child and whispered names back and forth as Urho worked silently. But between the babe's screams, Vale's whimpers when Urho's instruments pinched, and the sounds coming from down the hall in Caleb's room, there was still plenty of shouting going on.

With Tears Leaking down his face, Jason held Vale's still body in the bed, the breeze from the still-open window pouring over them. In the crevice between their forms, an equally still, tiny body rested, perfect and utterly beautiful.

With Vale's nose and dark hair. All ten fingers and toes.

And the sweetest breath that pulled in and out in little huffs that made Jason's heart ache.

Vale's steady breath was a delight as well. There had been a terrifying moment when blood seeped from Vale's body in copious amounts, and Jason had thought he might lose him. But Urho had gone in and sewn him up neatly, promising that Vale would live, that the babe would live.

And then Vale had declared them a family.

A family.

Jason hadn't been able to stop crying since then. All the tension and fear he'd held back through the majority of the pregnancy and then the labor let loose in a storm of emotion. Vale didn't blame him for it, because he was crying, too. And Urho couldn't tease or judge, because he'd gone on his way to help Xan with Caleb's heat. So, it was just him, his giant feelings, and his beautiful new family now.

He'd never thought they'd have this. Every moment since the birth was so perfect, beautiful, and raw. It almost hurt to hold so much joy in his arms.

Jason knew he should call his parents and tell them all had come to pass and that their son was perfect, and that Vale was strong. But he couldn't bring himself to get out of bed. He couldn't bring himself to stop staring at the miracles in his arms. His living *Erosgápe*. His beautiful son.

"What will we call him?" Vale's green eyes fluttered open, and his tired voice asked the question as if they'd been talking for the last few minutes. Another question among many.

"Oh, I don't know," Jason said, kissing Vale's eyelids, his nose, his bearded cheek, his mouth.

"Surely you've had something in mind?" Vale kissed Jason back. The tiny baby shifted between them, making soft suckling sounds in his sleep.

In all the months, Jason had refused to entertain the discussion of names, superstitious that if they gave the child a name too soon, they'd lose him. Or each other. "What about naming him for one of your parents?"

"Rupert and Dideon?" Vale shook his head. "I wouldn't want to saddle him with either of those names."

"Dido for short?" Jason offered.

"No. I was hoping for something more…"

"Poetic?"

Vale smiled. "Well, if I can't write poetry, at least I can give birth to it."

The baby twitched in his sleep, and Vale touched his tiny nose. Jason took a deep breath and ventured, "Virona?"

"Ah." Vale seemed to consider it. "After the place he was born."

"His eyes are sea-green."

"They're likely to change."

"No. They'll be like yours."

"You insist on it?"

Jason laughed.

Vale considered the name, smiled, and nodded. "Viro for short?"

Jason grinned. "I like that."

Little Viro opened his eyes then, demonstrating the truth of Jason's description, blinking black lashes over his stormy green eyes.

He opened his pink mouth, took a deep breath, and hollered with all the irritation of a confused pup.

Twittering with sudden nerves, Vale sat up, took him in his arms. Jason helped him get situated and helped to prop Viro's head as Vale placed him carefully to his nipple. They both smiled in awe as the baby took hold and fed. Jason watched eagerly, remembering the sweet taste of Vale's milk in his own mouth. "He'll grow up to be strong and brave."

An alpha's blessing for a first-born son.

"Urho thinks he'll be an alpha."

"Time will tell."

"Yes, we'll love him either way—beta, alpha. He's our son."

"Our beautiful boy," Jason agreed. "Wolf-god's blessing."

Viro and Vale were both safe and very much alive, and the fear that had consumed Jason and chipped away at his joy during the pregnancy lifted like a storm off the coast—blown out to sea.

Replaced by radiant sunlight.

EPILOGUE

V ALE CLUTCHED A sleeping Viro to his chest as the car bounced up the rough mountain road. The best thing about the baby was that he slept like a log once he was asleep. The worst thing about the baby was how very hard it was to get him to sleep to start with. Even now, the baby still slept in the bed with him and Jason because it was either that or not sleep at all from Viro's irritated fussing.

"Almost there," Jason said with a glance toward Vale and then down at his sleeping son. "He never sleeps this hard at home."

Vale kissed the top of Viro's head, his soft, almost-black curls tickling against Vale's lips. "Maybe we should take turns driving him around in the car for his naps."

Jason chuckled. "He doesn't like to sleep. He loves being alive."

"Of course, he does. He very much wanted to be here, after all. Insisted on it practically."

"Wolf-god wanted him here," Jason said, unusually devout when it came to Viro's presence in their lives. "Sent him despite our best efforts."

"Yes, I suppose he did."

Vale slipped his fingers into Viro's curls and closed his eyes to take in his son's compellingly wonderful scent. At six months, Viro was active, healthy, and if Vale did say so himself, a little bit wild. He was always pushing himself to go farther and faster than he really needed to go. He was a baby, after all, and destined to be Vale's only one at that, so did he really have to rush through everything?

It seemed so.

Viro was already sitting up, pulling himself to almost-standing, and determined to get his knees beneath him so that he could crawl. Their mess of a house back in the city was far from child-proofed, and Vale lived in a waking terror that Viro would get away from him somehow and get hurt before Vale could find him. And yet he and Jason were still too exhausted from the sleepless nights to figure out how to get the place in order.

That was the purpose of this visit to the mountain chalet after all. Miner and Yule were going to put the house to rights and get at least three rooms baby-safe. And while it pained Vale to imagine them going through his things and making choices about what to keep and what to put away in the basement, he knew he didn't have the energy or wherewithal to do it himself.

Being a pater was exhausting.

And beautiful. And the most compellingly captivating thing he'd ever done in his life. Aside from being with Jason, that is, as *Érosgápe* and lovers.

"You're quiet," Jason said as they made the last curve before they'd need to turn into the driveway. "Having regrets?"

"No," Vale said with a smile. He reached out and stroked Jason's thigh. "No regrets."

They'd talked about going to Jason's parents' house at Seshwan-by-the-Sea for this getaway, but in the end, Vale had suggested the cabin again. No one had been up to it since Jason's father had arranged to have the ruined car hauled off and the offending tree chopped into firewood. It was just past the anniversary of their ill-fated—if that term still applied—trip the prior year, and some part of Vale wanted to reclaim the place.

Jason had been a bit harder to convince, viewing the cabin as the scene of his failure to protect Vale from danger. But when Vale talked it up, reminding Jason that Viro was the blessing that came from that trip and that he wanted the boy to visit the place of his conception at least once before they sold the property, his baby alpha had, of course, caved.

"A week up here will be perfect for us," Vale said. "Your pater already sent someone up to baby-proof the place last week so that Viro will be safer here than at home."

"And Zephyr will get a break from him."

Vale pressed his smile against the top of Viro's little head. "Yes. Poor Zephyr."

Viro was obsessed with the cat and screeched with joy whenever Zephyr strolled into a room. Zephyr, for her part, was less enthusiastic about the wobbly, unpredictable, and loud creature who had invaded her home. She spent much of her time these days hiding in cupboards and avoiding the family.

"They'll become friends as he gets older," Jason asserted again for the thousandth time. "She'll see that Viro loves her."

Vale hoped he was right, but part of him suspected Zephyr would always despise Viro for stealing Vale's attentions, and Jason's comfortable lap.

"Ah," Jason said with a hint of lingering tension in his tone. They'd come through the tunnel of trees that made up the drive and pulled into the open space before the cottage. It looked very much like it had when they'd pulled up the first time—except for a massive stack of firewood against the side of the house, the remnants of the damnable tree that had taken out their car.

"It looks as if we'll be all set for any amount of snow and heat this time," Vale offered up with a touch of playfulness. If Jason was going to be solemn about this, then he'd have to break him out of it early. His baby alpha had felt guilty for too long. "Plenty of firewood, and a shockingly large box of alpha condoms." He shot Jason a sly look.

He wasn't kidding either. There was indeed a big box of alpha condoms in the trunk of the car. Chestfeeding would keep the heat at bay until Viro stopped nursing, but Jason wasn't taking any chances. Vale had barely restrained his laughter when he'd first seen the enormous box. "Darling, I'd have to be in heat every day of the rest of my life to need that many."

To which Jason had replied darkly, "I'll never let a residence of ours run low on condoms again. Better safe than sorry."

And Vale had let that go.

Though he wasn't sorry. Not at all. And, he knew, neither was Jason. Viro was worth all the fear and pain. But risking it again for a second child wasn't worth it to either of them—much to Yule and Miner's clear disappointment. But they made up for it in hogging Viro all they could. Which was part of the reason they were getting away to the cabin—to escape Vale's still-overbearing in-laws.

Jason got out first, walking around the car to open the door for Vale. He helped him out so that they didn't wake Viro, both of them marveling at the deep sleep of their usually restless child. Urho maintained it was evidence that the boy would likely present as an alpha eventually, but neither of them really cared. They just wanted him to sleep. And thrive. And grow up to be happy.

"It's too bad Rosen and Yosef couldn't join us after all," Vale said as Jason hefted the box of emergency condoms and grasped the handle of the biggest piece of luggage. They started toward the house. "Yosef is so good with Viro. And Rosen is so handy in the kitchen. He could have taken some of those responsibilities off your shoulders so you could truly rest."

"I can take care of my omega and child," Jason said defensively. "I don't need help."

Vale chuckled. "Of course, oh alpha, my alpha. You are the best provider in the world, and never need sleep or rest."

Jason sputtered, but Vale calmed him with a hot glance. "If this one keeps sleeping, we could see if the mattress is as soft as I remember."

Jason's exasperation vanished, replaced by a glimmer of interest.

"If we don't fall asleep first."

Vale lifted his chin, and Jason put down the luggage to grip it in his hand, fingers stroking Vale's beard. "We won't fall asleep, baby alpha," Vale said. "I've been missing you."

Jason got the front door of the cabin open quickly after that, though the sight of the living room and the sofa where he'd found Vale in such agony seemed to stop him in his tracks momentarily. But then he straightened his shoulders, put up his chin, and said, "I'll put the groceries away. You try to get him down. I'll meet you in the bedroom."

Vale nodded and shoved away his own memories of pain and desperation and the fear that had clouded their lives in the aftermath. Here was a beautiful view, and another, and a bedroom that was decorated with love. He took Viro into the guest room and noticed that at some point, Miner or Yule had arranged for a crib to be delivered. It took up the space along the inside wall, and Vale noted the sheets and fittings were sweet little gray cats with halos.

Carefully, with bated breath, he put Viro down in the crib. He bit into his lower lip and waited for the usual furious yell to rise up, but it didn't. Instead, Viro lay on his back, one small fist curled by his flushed face, his eyelashes black on his cheeks, and his hair curling sweetly all over his head. His breathing was steady and deep. His mouth pursed in a slight O. He was delicious-looking, and it was all Vale could do not to scoop him up again and cover him with kisses. But that would surely wake him up.

Carefully, he tiptoed from the room, and hearing the noise of Jason unboxing and unbagging things in the kitchen, Vale headed to the back bedroom and the large, glass wall that afforded the breath-taking view of the mountains. The bed was made nicely with the star-shaped quilt in the middle.

They hadn't left it like that.

When they'd finally been pulled off the mountain, they'd left the house a wreck behind them, too eager and shell-shocked to get home. But now it was tidy and beautiful again. He smoothed his hand over the quilt, touching the star in the middle, and then sat down on the bed to wait.

"He's actually asleep?" Jason asked, halting in the doorway with an expression of shock on his face. "Still?"

Vale nodded.

"I thought I'd find you chestfeeding him."

Vale shook his head.

Jason blinked, took in the room, glanced out the window, and then back at Vale. His expression going from startled and young to hot and very, very alpha in a flicker. "Why are your clothes still on?" He narrowed his gaze, an eyebrow going up. "Get them off. Now."

Vale grinned and reclined on the bed. "I thought you could do the honors."

"Oh, no," Jason said, his hands already working on his own shirt buttons. "I serviced you for months. You're going to service me now."

Vale's groin flooded with heat and warmth, and for the first time in months, his omega glands released slick. "Am I?"

"Yes," Jason growled. He glanced behind him and then closed the door until it was nearly shut, leaving it open just enough that they'd easily hear Viro if he cried. Or more like when he cried.

"Oh, darling, I like the sound of that."

"I know. I can smell you."

"Yes." He roughly pulled off his shirt and tossed it aside, and yanked down his pants, doing the same. His body looked different now. His hips were slightly wider, and his stomach skin wasn't as taut as before, but he was still attractive to Jason. He knew that in the way Jason's eyes raked over him, the stiffness of his cock as he approached the bed with his sharp, hungry smile.

"My beautiful man," Jason whispered, gathering Vale close and nuzzling against his beard. "My omega."

"Mm." He brushed his beard against Jason's neck and shoulders, making him shiver and moan. "Like that?"

"Get that mouth lower," Jason ordered. "You know what to do." He flopped on his back and spread his legs, and Vale crawled between them with a chuckle.

"Oh, I do know, yes." He rubbed his bearded chin over Jason's chest and nipples, stopping to lick and bite them gently, and then he rubbed it down lower against Jason's stomach, and finally over his hard cock and balls. Vale felt milk slip from his own nipples, and his cock was leaking, too. He felt like a shivery, wet mess of lust, what with the slick that dripped down his thighs.

"Fuck, baby," Jason muttered. "You're so sexy."

Vale grinned. He hadn't heard that in a few months. Beautiful, yes, amazing, yes, delicious, sweet, charming, lovely, handsome…yes, yes, yes. But sexy had been put aside for a while as he'd healed, and then Viro had sapped all their strength for too many weeks. He'd sucked Jason off a time or two, and let him reciprocate, but they'd not fully consummated their bond in the months since Viro's birth.

"I need you," he ventured, the usual omega bed-talk feeling rusty from disuse. "Help me."

Jason's eyes went dark with desire, and he reached out to guide Vale up for a kiss. They rolled on the bed together, naked, and lost in each other's skin and mouths. Finally, with Vale on top again, Jason urged him up to straddle his hips. "Ride me," he ordered breathlessly. "I want to look at you."

Vale settled back onto Jason's cock, both of them gasping as he took him straight to the root, a gush of wetness gliding the way. "Oh, fuck," Vale said as a small climax took him. It'd been too long.

Jason growled again and hunched up, dragging Vale down against him to kiss and cuddle, while fucking up into him slowly. The steady beat of his cock took Vale apart, and he cursed softly as pleasure swept over him.

Finally, all too soon, Jason flipped him over, dominating him entirely, fucking into him hard and fast, whispering in his ear, and Vale went flying. He came hard, his cock pumping fluid and his omega glands releasing slick as he cried out.

Jason grunted and thrust deep, holding tight as he came, too. His voice was roughened as he muttered his love, and Vale clung to him, digging his heels into Jason's ass, trying to hold him in deep.

"Ah-ah-ahhhhhhhhh!" Viro's voice split the air, and Jason huffed a laugh against Vale's shoulder.

"We barely made it," Jason said, pulling out slowly, and smirking as his cum spilled from Vale's body. "Oh, wow. Look at that."

"Just in time," Vale said breathlessly. "We finished just in time."

Jason scrambled for a towel to clean them up as Viro's protest at waking alone grew louder and louder. By the time Vale had his robe on, Jason was already down the hall, scooping the baby from his crib, and bringing him back to the master bedroom with him.

Vale snorted as Viro spotted him and reached out with chubby hands, his mouth already opening and closing in his demand for food. Jason passed him off and then went about replacing the sheets while Vale fed Viro in a chair next to the big, open window.

Viro stared off into the autumn view as he nursed, his mouth moving greedily, and his moss-green eyes taking in the changing leaves on the mountain with an intensity that Vale read as curiosity. One day soon, he'd try to write a poem about his son. For now, he was living the poem, minute by minute, day by day.

"No nap for us," Jason said with a sweet, satisfied smile. "He's going to be up for hours now."

"Yes. We should take him on a walk. Show him the view."

Jason nodded but then hesitated. "What if we see a bear?"

Vale smiled. "You'll protect us."

"From a bear?"

Vale laughed. "Don't worry, darling. Don't you know? The

danger is past us now. We made it past the challenge unscathed, and we're going to be all right from here on out."

Jason sank down at Vale's feet, looking up at him as Viro fed eagerly. His blue eyes filled with loving adoration. "We made him, Vale. You and me. Together."

"Yes. He's perfect." Restless and wild as he was, Vale wouldn't have his son any other way. Viro pointed toward the window and grunted. "Yes, we'll go out when you're done eating."

Jason went on as if they hadn't been interrupted. "And now we'll always be together in him. No matter what."

Vale leaned down to kiss Jason, barely interrupting Viro's greedy feeding. Finally, his alpha understood. This was why Vale hadn't been willing to end the pregnancy. But he stayed silent, enjoying the sensation of Jason's lips on his own.

Pulling away, Jason rested his head on Vale's knee, and the three of them sat together, looking at the mountains with the sky turning pink behind them. "This is perfect," Jason murmured. "I'm glad we came."

"Me, too."

Tomorrow would bring new challenges, no doubt, and more and more as Viro grew. But the danger was past. Viro existed. Vale was strong and healthy. Jason was happy, and their love was stronger than ever. And in a moment of clarity, Vale understood why he'd needed to return to this cabin in the woods. This was the place that had birthed their heart's desire almost against their will. And yet it held them beautifully now.

A small family silhouetted against a mountain sunset.

THE END

If you loved this story of Vale, Jason and baby Viro, and would like to read a bonus short scene from Vale's point of view, sign up for my newsletter and receive immediate access!

Letter from Leta

Dear Reader,

Thank you so much for reading *Slow Birth*, a novella in the *Heat of Love* series! To best enjoy this book, please read the first two books in the series, *Slow Heat* and *Alpha Heat*.

Extra stories for the *Heat of Love* series and other book universes can be found at my Patreon.

Be sure to follow me on BookBub or Amazon to be notified of new releases in this series and others. And look for me on Facebook for snippets of the day-to-day writing life. To see some sources of my inspiration, follow my Pinterest boards. I'm also on Instagram, so add me there, too!

If you enjoyed the book, please take a moment to leave a review! Reviews not only help readers determine if a book is for them, but also help a book show up in searches.

Also, for the audiobook connoisseur, the first two books in the series, *Slow Heat* and *Alpha Heat*, are available at most retailers that sell audio, narrated by the talented Michael Ferraiuolo.

Thank you for being a reader!
Leta

Book 1 in the Heat of Love series

SLOW HEAT

by Leta Blake

A lustful young alpha meets his match in an older omega with a past.

Professor Vale Aman has crafted a good life for himself. An unbonded omega in his mid-thirties, he's long since given up hope that he'll meet a compatible alpha, let alone his destined mate. He's fulfilled by his career, his poetry, his cat, and his friends.

When Jason Sabel, a much younger alpha, imprints on Vale in a shocking and public way, longings are ignited that can't be ignored. Fighting their strong sexual urges, Jason and Vale must agree to contract with each other before they can consummate their passion.

But for Vale, being with Jason means giving up his independence and placing his future in the hands of an untested alpha—as well as facing the scars of his own tumultuous past. He isn't sure it's worth it. But Jason isn't giving up his destined mate without a fight.

Book 2 in the Heat of Love series

ALPHA HEAT

by Leta Blake

A desperate young alpha. An older alpha with a hero complex. A forbidden love that can't be denied.

Young Xan Heelies knows he can never have what he truly wants: a passionate romance and happy-ever-after with another alpha. It's not only forbidden by the prevailing faith of the land, but such acts are illegal.

Urho Chase is a middle-aged alpha with a heartbreaking past. Careful, controlled, and steadfast, his friends dub him old-fashioned and staid. When Urho discovers a dangerous side to Xan's life that he never imagined, his world is rocked and he's consumed by desire. The carefully sewn seams that held him together after the loss of his omega and son come apart—and so does he.

But to love each other and make a life together, Xan and Urho risk utter ruin. With the acceptance and support of Caleb, Xan's asexual and aromantic omega and dear friend, they must find the strength to embrace danger and build the family they deserve.

Winter's Heart

Winter-fox always brings Tristan the best gifts

Tristan wakes every winter holiday to find a present that delights him or teaches him an important lesson.

Learn more about the character of Tristan, *Bitter Heat*'s Kerry and Janus's son, in this short winter holiday-themed story. This small bonus book doesn't contain the heat level of the full-length novels in this series, but it has all the cozy, hopeful warmth for a sweet holiday read. While it ends on a romantic note, the story does **not** contain a romance arc.

This story is **not a standalone** and is best read as an addition to the *Heat of Love* series, preferably after reading *Bitter Heat*. But if you should happen to read it out of order, you can find the rest of the books on Amazon and in Kindle Unlimited. *Another Heat of Love bonus novella by Leta Blake.*

Winter's Truth

Winter-fox brings Viro some surprising truths for the holiday

Viro Sabel is eleven years old and still entirely innocent about life. This year winter-fox brings him some surprising truths that alter the way he sees the world and his place in it.

Learn more about the character of Viro, *Slow Heat*'s Vale and Jason's son, in this **winter holiday-themed novella**. This medium-sized bonus book **features spicy scenes** between Vale and Jason, family scenes, and emotional moments. While the novella's epilogue teases a relationship for an adult Viro, it ends with a mystery regarding this person's identity.

This story is ***not* a standalone** and is best read as an addition to the *Heat of Love* series, preferably after reading *Slow Heat, Alpha Heat,* and *Slow Birth*. But if you should happen to read it out of order, you can find the rest of the books in the series on Amazon and in Kindle Unlimited.

HEAT FOR SALE
Heat can be sold but love is earned.

In a world where omegas sell their heats for profit, Adrien is a university student in need of funding. With no family to fall back on, he reluctantly allows the university's matcher to offer his virgin heat for auction online. Anxious, but aware this is the reality of life for all omegas, Adrien hopes whoever wins his heat will be kind.

Heath—a wealthy, older alpha—is rocked by the young man's resemblance to his dead lover, Nathan. When Heath discovers Adrien is Nathan's lost son from his first heat years before they met, he becomes obsessed with the idea of reclaiming a piece of Nathan.

Heath buys Adrien's heat with only one motivation: to impregnate Adrien, claim the child, and move on. But their undeniable passion shocks him. Adrien doesn't know what to make of the handsome, mysterious stranger he's pledged his body to, but he's soon swept away in the heat of the moment and surrenders to Heath entirely.

Once Adrien is pregnant, Heath secrets him away to his immense and secluded home. As the birth draws near, Heath grows to love Adrien for the man he is, not just for his connection to Nathan. Unaware of Heath's past with his omega parent and coming to depend on him heart and soul, Adrien begins to fall as well.

But as their love blossoms, Nathan's shadow looms. Can Heath keep his new love and the child they've made together once Adrien discovers his secrets?

Heat for Sale is a stand-alone m/m erotic romance by Leta Blake, writing as Blake Moreno. Infused with a du Maurier *Rebecca*-style secret, it features a well-realized omegaverse, an age-gap, dominance and submission, heats, knotting, and scorching hot scenes.

Gay Romance Newsletter

Leta's newsletter will keep you up to date on her latest releases and news from the world of M/M romance. Join the mailing list today and you're automatically entered into future giveaways.
letablake.com

Leta Blake on Patreon

Become part of Leta Blake's Patreon community in order to access exclusive content, deleted scenes, extras, bonus stories, rewards, prizes, interviews, and more.
www.patreon.com/letablake

Other Books by Leta Blake

Contemporary

Will & Patrick Wake Up Married
Will & Patrick's Endless Honeymoon
Cowboy Seeks Husband
The Difference Between
Bring on Forever
Stay Lucky

Sports

The River Leith

The Training Season Series
Training Season
Training Complex

Musicians

Smoky Mountain Dreams
Vespertine

New Adult

Punching the V-Card

Winter Holidays

The Home for the Holidays Series
Mr. Frosty Pants
Mr. Naughty List
Mr. Jingle Bells

Fantasy

Any Given Lifetime

Re-imagined Fairy Tales

Flight
Levity

Paranormal & Shifters

Angel Undone
Omega Mine

Horror

Raise Up Heart

Omegaverse

Heat of Love Series
Slow Heat
Alpha Heat
Slow Birth
Bitter Heat

For Sale Series
Heat for Sale

Coming of Age

'90s Coming of Age Series
Pictures of You
You Are Not Me

Audiobooks

Leta Blake at Audible

Discover more about the author online

Leta Blake
letablake.com

About the Author

Author of the bestselling book *Smoky Mountain Dreams* and the fan favorite Omegaverse series *Heat of Love*, Leta Blake's educational and professional background is in psychology and finance, respectively. However, her passion has always been for writing. She enjoys crafting romance stories and exploring the psyches of imaginary people. At home in the Southern U.S., Leta works hard at achieving balance between her writing and her family life.